"You'd like to know about Corina, wouldn't you?"

George spoke blandly. Phoebe answered a little wildly, "No, I wouldn't!" she lied. "I'm not in the least bit interested. Anyway, it's all so obvious. I mean, she's an old friend, isn't she? You must enjoy meeting her again." Her tongue ran on quite ridiculously. "She's so pretty and... It's all such a waste of time, isn't it? And I think I'm tired after all."

She sprang from the chair and skidded across the room on her shoeless feet and ran upstairs at a great rate, just as though she expected George to run after her.

Only he didn't.

Books by Betty Neels

HARLEQUIN ROMANCE

These books may be available at your local bookseller.

Don't miss any of our special offers. Write to us at the following address for information on our newest releases.

Harlequin Reader Service
P.O. Box 52040, Phoenix, AZ 85072-2040
Canadian address: P.O. Box 2800, Postal Station A,
5170 Yonge St., Willowdale, Ont. M2N 6J3

A Summer Idyll

Betty Neels

Harlequin Books

TORONTO • NEW YORK • LONDON
AMSTERDAM • PARIS • SYDNEY • HAMBURG
STOCKHOLM • ATHENS • TOKYO • MILAN

Original hardcover edition published in 1984
by Mills & Boon Limited

ISBN 0-373-02712-5

Harlequin Romance first edition August 1985

CHAPTER ONE

IT was quite ten minutes after a ragged chorus of church bells had tolled the hour of five before Phoebe tapped on the office door and, when bidden, entered. Sister Evans was at her desk, looking as fierce as usual, and without glancing up she asked briskly: 'Yes, what is it?'

Phoebe didn't allow the eagerness she felt to sound in her voice. 'I've finished, Sister—I'm off at five o'clock.'

'Very well, Nurse Creswell.' It was a surprised Phoebe who heard Sister wish her a pleasant evening. She thanked her politely and whisked herself out of the office and back down the ward. Almost at the doors old Mrs James sat up in bed. 'Nurse, nurse—I feel sick!'

There wasn't another nurse to be seen. Busy in the sluice or the kitchen or even having a cosy chat in the linen cupboard—it was such a safe time on a medical ward, not time for evening medicines, far too early for the getting ready of suppers, a most unlikely hour for a houseman to do a round and Sister safe in her office. Phoebe sighed, nipped into the sluice room for a bowl and hurried back with it. Just my luck, she thought silently, proffering it and arranging a towel in a strategic place, just when she needed at least an hour to get ready before Basil expected her. A precious ten minutes went by before Mrs James decided that she felt better and consented to be tucked up once more.

The hospital, hedged in by East End streets lined with small grey houses, was old, added to

5

from time to time, regardless of level floors or unnecessary staircases, so that Phoebe was quite out of breath by the time she reached her room in the nurses' home, a state not helped by the speed in which she flung off her uniform, showered and then began to dress. She had given a good deal of thought to what she should wear, Basil had mentioned casually that the party was being given by a cousin of his—a real swinger, he had called her, and possessed of stunning good looks. Phoebe, surveying her own very ordinary features in the mirror, wished wholeheartedly that the cousin would spare some of her good looks for her. There was nothing wrong with her face, she supposed, but it would never set the world on fire. And mousy hair did nothing to help, and since no one had ever pointed out that her eyes were beautiful, grey and heavily fringed, she set no great store by them. She sat down and did her face and then her hair, twisting it up in a neat knot and pinning it carefully before getting into the new separates she had bought in the January sales, a pleasant shade of green and of a fine jersey, just right for a spring evening. She had only been out with Basil three times, and she was still secretly surprised that she was going out with him and that he seemed to like her. He was one of the most popular housemen and could have taken his pick of any number of girls far prettier than she. He was good-looking too, and never at a loss for conversation. Phoebe thought he was marvellous, and she had a perpetual daydream, in which he fell in love with her, married her and became a successful consultant with a Harley Street practice with her running a flat-fronted Regency house and entertaining his rich patients in a little something from Bellville Sassoon. Nonsense, she told herself firmly several times a day, while a tiny corner of her mind persisted in denying that.

She put on the plain court shoes she had saved to buy, found her velvet jacket and, with a couple of minutes to spare, made her way round to the car park at the back of the hospital where the staff kept their cars.

Basil's car was there—an elderly Triumph, its vivid red needing a good clean—but Basil wasn't; he was at the other end of the row of cars, leaning on the bonnet of a sleek Rover, talking to Staff Nurse Collins whose father was well-heeled enough to keep his daughter in a style quite inaccessible to a nurse living on nothing but her pay. Phoebe stayed where she was, not sure whether to join them or look as though she hadn't seen them. She decided on the latter, and presently was relieved to hear Basil's voice remarking that there she was and why hadn't she given a shout.

She mumbled something or other, bereft of words as usual when she was with him, although her smile made up for that, and when he opened the car door, she got in. She had hoped he would say something nice about her outfit, but he hardly glanced at it, merely said that they would have to step on it if they weren't to miss the best of the food.

The cousin lived miles away, near Croydon. What with Basil taking a wrong turning and all the evening traffic, the party was in full swing by the time he had found a place to park the car and they had walked back to the rather staid-looking house in a quiet street. Although neither the house nor the street were quiet; the din met them as they opened the old-fashioned iron gate and pushed open the half-open door.

The moment they were inside, Phoebe saw that

she was dressed quite wrongly; there were dozens of girls there, wearing slinky black dresses with deep vee necklines and no backs worth mentioning, and those who weren't wearing black were in tight pant suits, glittering with gold and sequins. The girl who came to meet them was wearing black satin, skin tight and short; she wore one very large dangling earring and there were pink streaks in her dark hair. She flung her arms round Basil, kissed him with great warmth and then looked at Phoebe. 'Girl-friend?' she enquired, 'Basil, I can't believe it?'

The amused look she cast at Phoebe sent the colour flying into her cheeks, and it stayed there because Basil looked at her too with a faint derisive smile. 'Hardly that,' he said, but he took Phoebe's arm and squeezed it, and the smile changed so quickly that she thought that she might have imagined it.

The girl grinned, 'I'm Deirdre,' and when Phoebe said politely: 'How do you do? I'm Phoebe,' she said rather impatiently: 'Well, come on in and meet everyone.' Somebody went past with a tray of drinks and she caught him by the arm. 'Have a drink for a start.'

It tasted like sugared petrol, but Phoebe sipped it obediently, keeping close to Basil because she didn't know a soul there. True, he threw names at her carelessly from time to time, but faces came and went so rapidly that she never caught up with them. And presently she found herself against a wall and Basil at the other end of the room surrounded by a crowd of people all laughing their heads off. She had hidden her glass behind a great vase filled with lilac and was trying to look as though she was enjoying herself; not that that mattered, because no one noticed her. It seemed like hours later when Basil reappeared, a glass in his hand. 'Hullo there,' he began carelessly. 'Having a good time? I say, this is some party—haven't enjoyed myself so much in years.' He looked at her and frowned. 'You look a bit of a wet blanket, darling—it's not quite your scene, perhaps.'

She was anxious to please him. 'Oh, it's lovely,' she assured him. 'I came here just for a minute or two, to get my breath.'

He dropped a casual kiss on her cheek. 'Oh, good. There's masses of food in the other room, but I daresay you've had all you want.'

He slid away, leaving her with her mouth watering; she was famished, now that she came to think about it. Hunger sent her edging her way through the people milling round the room. She found a plate and collected tiny sausage rolls, smoked salmon on slivers of brown bread and butter, tiny vol-au-vents, a stick of celery—hardly a meal, but it would keep her empty insides quiet for a little while—then she found a chair in a corner of the room, and was surprised when presently she was joined by another of the guests. A thin, pale man, in a good grey suit, looking, she had to admit, as much like a fish out of water as she did.

'On your own?' he asked.

'No, but I've—that is, the man I came with has heaps of friends here—and of course he wants to talk to them.'

He gave her a long considered look. 'Not quite your sort,' he commented. 'Not mine either—a lot of layabouts with too much money and nothing to do. You look as though you earn your own living?'

It was hardly a compliment, but it was so nice to

talk to someone that she felt no resentment. 'Yes, I'm training to be a nurse.'

'Good Lord—who did you come with?'

'Basil Needham. He's a houseman at St Coram's.'

Her companion said, 'Good Lord,' again, and gave her another faintly pitying look. 'I'd never have believed it of him.'

She misunderstood him and said earnestly: 'Oh, he's very clever—I expect he'll be famous one day.' Her eyes shone with delight at such a prospect and the man looked vaguely uncomfortable.

'Not very old, are you?' he observed.

'Twenty-two.' She looked around her. 'Are people beginning to go? I must find Basil . . .'

'Oh, they'll go to a night club.'

'Well, I'll have to find him just the same—we'll have to get back to St Coram's.' She added politely: 'It's been nice meeting you. I expect you're going to a night club too.'

He got to his feet. 'God forbid—I live here.' He walked away, leaving her gaping after him, and then she forgot him as Basil pushed his way through the people leaving.

'There you are. We're all going on to a disco . . .'

Phoebe wasn't listening. 'Who was that man?' she asked. 'He said he lived here.'

'Well, of course he does, you little idiot, he's Deirdre's husband. Get your coat—it'll be a bit of a squash in the car, but that won't matter.'

'We're going back to St Coram's?'

He gave her an impatient look. 'Good God, no! Do get a move on.'

Phoebe, a mild-tempered girl, didn't budge. 'I'm not coming,' she said mulishly.

'Don't be a fool! You've no way of getting back on your own.'

Which was true enough. She had thrust a handful of small change into her purse, probably not enough to get her back to St Coram's. Her mind boggled at the long walk ahead of her, even if she could get a bus for part of the way.

'If you could lend me some money for a taxi?' she suggested diffidently.

'No way. I'll need all I've got with me. Get a bus.' Just for a moment Basil looked uncertain. 'You won't change your mind?'

She shook her head, willing him to change his, but he didn't; he turned on his heel and left her without so much as a backward glance. After a minute or so Phoebe followed him, to find the hall empty. She picked up her coat for a moment, pausing, then put it on and went to the door. She was on the point of going through it when the man she had spoken to during the evening came into the hall.

'Everyone gone?'

'Yes. I'm just . . . that is . . . thank you for a nice party.'

'Not going to the disco?'

'Well, no. I'm going to catch a bus . . .'

He had come to stand beside her. 'I'll drive you back to your hospital.' He muttered something under his breath, it sounded like, 'It's the least I can do.' But she wasn't sure of that.

Phoebe said politely: 'It's very kind of you to offer, but you have no need.'

For answer he took her arm, banged the door behind them and crossed the pavement to a Mercedes parked at the kerb. Phoebe got in, since there seemed no point in protesting further, and was whisked across London without further ado. Her companion didn't say a word until they had reached the hospital, and when she thanked him he said carelessly: 'Not at all. I'd better go and look for my wife, I suppose.'

Phoebe couldn't think of anything suitable to reply to this; she murmured goodnight and smiled uncertainly. It surprised her very much when he leaned across to say to her: 'Give him up, my dear—he's not for you.'

He had driven away before she could think of an answer to that one too.

And it seemed as though he would be right. Phoebe didn't see Basil at all the following day— nor, for that matter, for several days to come. And when at last she met him face to face as she came back from the Path. Lab. he gave her a cool nod and would have walked right past her if she hadn't stopped him with a firm voice which surprised her as much as it surprised him.

'Didn't you worry?' she asked. 'Leaving me to get back on my own from that party?'

He flushed a little. 'Worry? Why should I worry? A sensible girl like you—you're hardly likely to attract unwelcome attentions, are you?'

His faint sneer made her wince, but all the same she asked: 'Why not?'

She knew the answer; she supposed that because she had thought that she was in love with him, it was going to hurt, however nicely he put it.

But he didn't bother with niceness. 'My dear girl, you're not silly enough to imagine you're pretty?'

'Then why did you take me out?'

Basil laughed. 'An experience, shall we say—a very unrewarding one, I might add.'

Phoebe didn't say anything to that: she stood on tiptoe in her sensible black shoes and smacked his cheek hard. She was appalled the moment she had done it; it was an unpardonable thing to do, she told herself as she bolted back to the ward, to find

Sister irate at the length of time she had been away. She stood meekly before that lady, letting her run on and on, and then, impatiently dismissed, skipped back to the ward to her endless chores.

There was an auxiliary nurse off sick, which meant that there was even more to do than usual; she steadily trotted to and fro, getting hot and untidy, responding to her patients' wants, glad at the same time that she had so much to occupy her that there was precious little time to think. Only when she was off duty did she allow her thoughts to dwell on Basil—a broken dream, she admitted that honestly, and she had been a fool to indulge in it. He'd been amusing himself between girl-friends, she had no doubt—like eating a slice of bread and butter between rich cream cakes.

She sat down at her functional dressing table, took off her cap and studied her face. Presently she unpinned her hair and pushed it this way and that, judging the effect. It was no good—she remained, at least to the casual eye, uninteresting. In her dressing gown presently, she trailed along the corridor and joined her friends over tea and a gossip, while at the back of her mind the idea of leaving—going right away—was already forming. She could give a month's notice and start again at another hospital. It would be a wrench, because she had been happy during the last year; she was never going to be brilliant in the nursing world, but she was good with patients and kind and gentle. Besides, she was young enough to start again. The idea had solidified into certainty by the time she was in bed; a fresh start, and she would forget the hurt Basil had inflicted.

She slept soundly because she was tired, but when she woke she knew that her mind was made up. She would go that very morning and see the Principal Nursing Officer, something she hardly looked forward to, as that lady was known among the lesser fry at the hospital as the Tartar—a quite unsuitable name, as it happened, for she was by no means fiery in character, although her wooden expression, and the fact that she smiled only at Christmas and the Annual Ball, made her intimidating. But Phoebe, having decided, wasn't going to be put off by that. When the breakfasts had been served and Sister had come on duty, she knocked on the office door, ready with her request to go to the office at nine o'clock.

But the speech was unnecessary. Sister looked up as she went in. 'They've just rung through, Nurse—you're to go down to the office at once. Run along.'

Phoebe didn't run, mindful of Sister Tutor's remarks about fire and haemorrhage, but she walked very fast, wondering what on earth she'd done.

She put an anxious hand to her cap, knocked on the door and was bidden to go in. The Tartar's wooden features wore an expression which Phoebe could only imagine to be sympathy, although she spoke briskly enough.

'Nurse Creswell, your aunt, Miss Kate Mason, is ill. She has asked her doctor to send for you— apparently you are her only relative.' She gave Phoebe an accusing look as though that was her fault. 'She feels most strongly that your place is by her side so she may be nursed back to health. I should add, Nurse, that your aunt is suffering from chronic bronchitis and crippling arthritis and is unlikely to regain a state of health when she will be unable to do without your care. It means, of course, that you will have to give up your training for at least the immediate future.'

Phoebe stared at the Tartar's cold eyes while she digested this information. Here was help—not quite what she would have wished for, but a loophole of escape. Aunt Kate was a holy terror; dictatorial and on the mean side, she had ignored her family for years and Phoebe, the last member of it left, hadn't seen her for some time. So like Aunt Kate, she mused, to turn a cold shoulder on the family and then demand help as though it was her right. But it was an escape . . .

'Am I to go at once, Miss Ratcliffe?'

'Naturally. I consider this an emergency and the doctor who is attending her stresses the need for nursing help as soon as possible. You will be given compassionate leave until your leaving date and you will, of course, receive payment until that day. You may go today, Nurse Creswell, and I trust that your year with us as a student nurse has given you a good grounding for whatever tasks you will need to undertake.'

Phoebe sorted this out. 'Yes, Miss Ratcliffe, I'll do my best.' She added rather shyly: 'I've been very happy here.'

The Tartar inclined her head graciously.'I trust that your future will be as happy, Nurse. Goodbye.'

Very doubtful, thought Phoebe, speeding back to the ward to tell Sister. Aunt Kate lived in Suffolk, in a village which she remembered only vaguely—but even if it had been a large town, she doubted very much whether she would get a great deal of time to spare. All the same, she liked the country; she would use some of her savings to buy a bike, so that when she had an hour or so . . . She was already making the best of a bad job when she knocked once more on Sister's door.

Sister was surprised and flatteringly reluctant to

let her go. 'Not that I can do much about it,' she grumbled. 'I quite see that if your aunt has no one else to look after her, there's nothing else to be done.'

Phoebe refrained from saying that Aunt Kate had sufficient money to employ a private nurse if she so wished.

'Well, you'd better go,' sighed Sister, 'and you were turning into quite a good nurse too.'

Phoebe bade her goodbye, announced her departure to the nurses on the ward, explained to the patients, and took herself off to her room, where she started to pack. She was about halfway through this when two of her friends came over to change their aprons. They listened to her with astonishment, heedless of returning to their wards, begged her to write, and promised to say goodbye on her behalf to her other friends.

'What about Basil?' one of them asked.

Phoebe bent over her case, ramming things in with some force. 'I've had no time to see him or let him know,' she said casually. 'I daresay we'll meet up some time.'

Her companions exchanged glances. 'Well, have fun, Phoebe—we shall miss you.'

She would miss them too, she thought, sitting in the train, gazing out at the flat Essex countryside, but perhaps she would make new friends in the village. It was quite a long journey, and by the time the train reached Stowmarket, she was famished. She put her two cases in the left luggage at the station, then went into a nearby café and had a meal of sorts before collecting her luggage once more and crossing the square to board the bus for Woolpit. It was a five-mile ride and Phoebe sat in the almost empty bus, watching the first signs of spring with delight. London's parks were all very well, but they couldn't compete with primroses and the bread-and-cheese in the hedges under a thin sunshine from a pale blue sky. The bus turned off the by pass, rattled down the narrow road to the village and stopped at one side of the village green. Aunt Kate's house was on the other side, beyond the village pump, a nice old house with sash windows and tall Tudor chimneys. Phoebe said goodbye to the driver and carried her cases across the green, put them down in the porch which sheltered the white wood door, and thumped the knocker. The Tartar had told her that she would telephone the doctor to say that Phoebe was coming at once, but she doubted if she was expected quite as soon.

The door opened cautiously and a girl of sixteen peered round it.

'Hullo,' said Phoebe, 'I've come to look after Miss Mason. May I come in? I'm expected.'

The girl smiled then. She opened the door wide, took one of Phoebe's cases from her and said breathlessly: 'Oh, miss, come in, do. I said I'd stay until you got 'ere, 'e said I was to, but now I can go 'ome.'

'Do you come each day?' asked Phoebe quickly. 'And what's your name?'

'Susan, and I come mornings, to clean and that—there's been a nurse, but she won't come no more—couldn't manage with Miss Mason's ways. Went this morning, early she did.'

Hence the urgency, thought Phoebe. The doctor, whoever he might be, must think of her as a gift from heaven. She could imagine his relief; being a niece of his troublesome patient, she could hardly pack her bags and leave.

'Well, I'm here now,' said Phoebe hearteningly. 'Just show me where my room is and where you keep everything. Is my aunt in bed? Asleep?'

Susan nodded. 'She usually has a nap till tea.'
She added anxiously. 'We could be quiet like.'

Phoebe nodded in wholehearted agreement. Let
her just have time to look around her and make a
cup of tea, she prayed hopefully, and followed
Susan down the hall.

She remembered the house well enough. The
kitchen was at the right of the passage at the back,
a roomy old-fashioned place, its only concession
to modern times being the gas stove. Aunt Kate
had never seen the sense in spending money on
washing machines and the like when she could get
a young local girl to do the chores for a small
wage. All the same, it was a pleasant place as well
as old-fashioned, and it was clean. Phoebe nodded
understanding at Susan's pointing finger; the larder,
the sink, the various drawers and the old-
fashioned dresser. They went quietly out again and
disregarded the sitting room and dining room
doors, then crept up the stairs beside the back
door. The landing was roomy and had four doors
leading from it as well as a narrow stair leading to
the attics. One door was closed, and they listened
long enough to hear the snores from behind it and
then crossed to one of the rooms at the front of
the house. It was rather sparsely furnished and the
curtains and bed spread were a depressingly dull
green, but it overlooked the street and the pale sun
made it cheerful. A vase of flowers, thought
Phoebe, and her few bits and pieces scattered
around, would make all the difference. She nodded
to Susan, took off her coat and left it on the bed and
accompanied her silently downstairs again.

'Tomorrow?' she asked.

Susan nodded. 'Ar past eight, miss, till 'ar past
twelve.' She was putting on her coat. 'There's

things for supper in the larder—eggs and that.'

Phoebe opened the door, wished her goodbye and closed it quietly. Tea first, she decided, and something to eat. She was famished again, and once Aunt Kate woke she would probably be kept busy.

She put the kettle on, found teapot, tea, a bottle of milk and the sugar bowl and half a packet of digestive biscuits, and presently sat down at the table. It wasn't much of a meal, but she felt all the better for it and after she had tidied up she poked her head into the larder and assessed its contents. Eggs, some fish on a plate—but only enough for one—bread in the bin, butter, some old cheese and nothing much else. She wondered what the nurse had had to eat, and what, for that matter, she was to eat herself. The cupboards yielded a good supply of flour and oats and rice and sugar though; given time she should be able to whip up some sort of meal for the invalid. She found a tray and put it ready in case Aunt Kate should wake. It was well after four o'clock and perhaps she should take a look.

There was no need, a bell tinkled urgently and Phoebe hurried up the stairs, tapped on her aunt's door and went in.

Aunt Kate was propped up in bed, swathed in a thick shawl and by no means in a good temper. 'So there you are,' she snapped between coughs. 'And high time too—when a body can't depend on her own kith and kin taking care of her it's a poor state of affairs. I don't know what the world's coming to!'

Phoebe didn't know either, and since Aunt Kate's remarks were exactly the same as the last time they had met, she said merely: 'I came as soon as the hospital had your message, Aunt Kate, I'm sorry you are ill.'

'Pooh,' said Aunt Kate strongly. 'Fiddlesticks—
and don't think you'll get a penny piece from me, my
girl—I've better ways of leaving my money.' She
added quickly: 'Not that I have any money, living
here on my own with no one to bother about me.'

'The nurse?' asked Phoebe.

'Bah—stupid woman, all she could think of was
her meals.' She shot Phoebe a grumpy look, her
dark little eyes half closed. 'Do you eat a lot?'

'Yes,' said Phoebe simply. 'Would you like your
tea now?'

Aunt Kate had a fit of coughing. 'Yes—thin
bread and butter with it. When I've had it I'll talk
to you.'

It was hard to be sorry for the old lady; she was
ill and crippled with arthritis, and Phoebe did her
best to pity her as she went back to the kitchen.
She made the tea, cut paper-thin bread and butter
and at the same time made jam sandwiches for
herself, since she was still hungry, and having
settled her aunt against her pillows with the tea
tray on the bed table, went down again to make
another pot of tea to accompany the sandwiches.
She had just finished the last of them when Aunt
Kate rang the bell.

'You'll stay of course,' she began without
preamble. 'You're my niece, my great-niece, and
it's your duty.'

'I've been training as a nurse,' observed Phoebe
mildly.

'Time enough for that after I've gone. I'll not
last long—that Dr Pritchard says I'm good for
a few more years yet, but I know better.'

'What happened to Dr Bennett?' asked Phoebe,
vaguely remembering a small neat man with a
goatee beard who called Aunt Kate 'dear lady' and
sometimes had stayed for tea.

'Retired, drat him. Now I have to bear with this little whipper-snapper who takes no notice of me whatsoever.' Aunt Kate pushed the bed table away impatiently. 'You can take this; I'll have a bit of fish for my supper—done in milk, mind—and an egg custard.'

Phoebe took the bed table away and picked up the tray. 'Tomorrow,' she said with firm gentleness, 'perhaps you will give me some money and I'll buy some food. There's almost nothing to eat in the house.'

'My appetite's poor,' snapped Aunt Kate.

'I expect so, but mine isn't. If I'm to stay, Aunt Kate, then I shall want to be fed, and since I've no money of my own, I'm afraid you'll have to pay me a salary.'

The old lady's eyes snapped. 'My own niece demanding a salary?'

'That's right. After all, you had to pay the nurse, didn't you? Private nurses are very expensive.'

Aunt Kate mumbled something in a cross voice and Phoebe was given to understand that she would be given pocket money—the sum mentioned would buy toothpaste and shampoo and tights, but precious little else, but Phoebe was satisfied. It was, after all, a small declaration of independence; if she hadn't taken a stand then and there, she would have become a doormat.

She took the tea tray downstairs and went back again to wash her aunt's face and hands and make her bed, chatting cheerfully as she did so. The doctor, her aunt told her grudgingly, came in the morning after surgery; it was he who had insisted on her having a nurse after calling unexpectedly one afternoon and finding her out of bed and struggling to get downstairs to get herself a meal.

'Why not the district nurse?' asked Phoebe.

'Won't have her near me,' declared Aunt Kate, and Phoebe sighed; the old lady took fierce dislikes to some people and no amount of inconvenience to other people would alter that. 'Nothing more than a baggage, that nurse Dr Pritchard made me have. Always looking at herself in the glass, wanting time off, if you please, said she needed recreation.' Aunt Kate gave a weary little snort. 'As though she had anything to do here! Susan cleans the house.'

Phoebe held her tongue and then asked what time she wanted her supper.

'Half past seven, and no later. And mind you do that fish in milk.'

Phoebe left a bedside light on, laid spectacles, book, handkerchief and bell within reach and took herself off to the kitchen. The fish looked unappetising; a morsel of creamed potato might brighten it up a bit, and she could purée a few carrots.

She had just set the egg custard in its pan of warm water when the front door was opened. Susan couldn't have closed it properly and she hadn't bothered to look herself. It might be a neighbour, but she doubted that; Aunt Kate didn't encourage neighbours; she ought to go into the hall and see who it was, but if she did, the custard might spoil if she didn't get it into the oven at once.

Her decision was made for her. The kitchen door, half open, was flung wide and a large man came in. He was tall as well as broad with fair hair, cut short, a handsome face and a decidedly brisk manner.

'So you got here,' he stated with satisfaction. 'Thought I'd make sure you had arrived, otherwise it would have been the district nurse and fireworks. What's your name?'

'Phoebe Creswell.' Phoebe frowned. 'What's yours?'

'Pritchard, George.' He held out a hand and smiled and she didn't feel put out any more; he had a smile which was nice, friendly and reassuring. 'I hope your aunt is pleased to see you.'

Phoebe closed the door gently on the custard. 'Well, yes, I think on the whole she is.'

He nodded. 'Good. She's ill, you know that.' His gaze swept round the kitchen and stayed on the fish. 'Her supper?' he wanted to know. 'What about you?'

She was touched that he had thought of that. 'Well, there's nothing much in the house—I can't think what the nurse had to eat. I'll make some toasted cheese.' The small nose twitched; she was hungry again. After all, she hadn't had much to eat all day—a good cooked dinner. Her mouth watered at the thought.

'I'm on the other side of the green. When I've done my rounds I'll send my housekeeper over to sit here while you have supper with me. No, don't argue, it'll give me a chance to explain your aunt's case to you and discuss medicines and so on.' He glanced at his watch. 'About eight o'clock. Right?'

Phoebe nodded happily. If this was Aunt Kate's little whipper-snapper then she liked him. She closed the door after him and went back to her cooking. Life was suddenly full of promise. She hadn't thought of Basil even once.

CHAPTER TWO

AUNT KATE, while showing no gratitude for her supper, ate all of it, reminded Phoebe that she would have a glass of hot milk at nine o'clock precisely and told her grudgingly that she might go downstairs and eat her own meal. But first she needed her pillows shaken up, her spectacles, glass of water, and the local newspaper. Only then did she add: 'At least your cooking is passable, and don't forget my milk.' She added: 'I shall be perfectly all right for an hour or so. When you've cleared up you can unpack your things.'

'Yes, Aunt Kate.' Phoebe spoke mildly, her thoughts on supper.

She had had the forethought to leave the front door on the latch, and before she had done more than clear the tray, a thin elderly woman came quietly in. She was dressed in a thick skirt and a grey cardigan, which, with her pepper-and-salt hair cut severely short and her pale face, gave Phoebe the impression that she was looking at an etching. They shook hands and she changed her mind. Mrs Thirsk had the bluest eyes she had ever met, and when she smiled her whole face lit up.

'Supper's on the table, Miss . . .'

'Call me Phoebe, please, Mrs Thirsk.'

'Phoebe.' The smile came and went again. 'But I'll just see to these . . .'

'You leave them. The doctor said you were to go straight over.' She studied Phoebe's small, too thin figure. 'You look as though you could do with a good hot meal.'

'Oh, I could—there's been no time . . .'

'And nothing in the house, I'll be bound.' Mrs Thirsk went to the sink and filled the bowl with water from the kettle. 'I've brought my knitting,' she stated. 'Take your jacket, it's chilly.'

Phoebe nodded, slung her cardigan over her shoulders and went out of the house, across the green, to tap on the solid wooden door of the doctor's house. It was a good deal grander than her aunt's, of white bricks, with a tiled roof and Elizabethan chimneypots to match and latticed windows. She stood back to get a better view just as the door was opened.

'Come in,' invited Dr Pritchard, 'it's rabbit stew with dumplings—one of Mrs Thirsk's masterpieces.'

The hall was square, with a curved staircase to one side of it and several doors leading from it. The floor was of flagstones covered for the most part with rugs with a carved chest along one wall. A large black labrador pranced to meet Phoebe as she went in, sniffed her fist and barked cheerfully.

'Beauty,' said Dr Pritchard, 'I hope you like dogs?'

'Oh, yes, but I've never had one of my own.' She gave him a rather shy smile. 'I like cats too.'

'In the kitchen,' he said briefly, 'a basket full of them; Venus has just had kittens.'

He pushed open one of the doors and she went past him into the sitting room, a low-ceilinged, beamed and cosily furnished room, with chairs pulled up to the log fire in the wide hearth.

'You could do with a glass of sherry,' stated the doctor, and handed her one before she could answer. 'Do sit down.'

They didn't talk much as they had their drinks, only a few questions and answers; how long was it

since she had been there? How far was she with her
training? Did she intend to resume that later on?

To all of which she replied a little vaguely, since
she hadn't really thought about it yet. And over
supper the doctor kept the conversation on general
topics while they ate with healthy appetites. It was
only when they had carried the dishes to the
kitchen, admired Venus and her kittens and taken
the coffee tray into the sitting room that he started
to tell her about Aunt Kate.

'Of course, she can't last out much longer,' he
explained. 'She's worn out and her heart is already
weak. I've done what I can, but she refuses to go
into hospital or a nursing home and the nurse I
arranged for was given short shrift. How about
you? You've not had much to say so far.'

'Well, I've not had much time to think about it,
have I? Phoebe's quiet face was turned to the fire. 'Of
course, I shall stay even if Aunt Kate dislikes it, and
she will in a few days, even though she insisted on my
coming. She's never liked anyone in the family and
I'm the only one left now. She says it's my duty.'

She glanced at the doctor watching her intently.
'There's nothing else to do,' she added simply. 'But
I'd much rather not.'

'Any ties?' he asked idly, and when she looked
puzzled. 'Boy-friends and so forth?'

Phoebe went pink. 'No.' She had the urge to tell
him all about Basil and how coming to Aunt
Kate's had solved that problem for her, but after
all, she had only just met him. When she didn't say
anything he said slowly: 'Well, that makes things
easier, doesn't it? Now, as to treatment . . .'

He was all at once the doctor.

'When he had finished she said: 'I'll do my best,
Dr Pritchard. Do you come every day to see
Aunt Kate?'

'Oh, yes. Just a quick check-up, you know.' He smiled at her very kindly. 'And don't forget to pass on any problems, however small.'

It seemed the right moment to go and he made no effort to keep her, but walked across the green to her aunt's door and waited until Mrs Thirsk opened it, said a few brief words to Phoebe and went back with her. Phoebe, closing the door slowly, watched them go, comforted by the fact that they were within shouting distance.

Aunt Kate was sitting up in bed reading. As Phoebe went in she looked up and asked: 'My milk—is it ready? It's more than time—and I have some pills to take.'

'Yes, Aunt, I'll fetch the milk now and your pills. Is there anything I can do for you before you have them?'

Aunt Kate rapped out a list of small wants. 'And mind you lock up properly,' she ended breathlessly. 'I never trusted that other creature.' She fell into a fit of coughing and finally gasped crossly: 'For heaven's sake, Phoebe, don't just stand there!'

It took almost an hour to settle Aunt Kate for the night. When she was at last satisfied that everything had been done to her satisfaction, she lay back against her pillows, allowed Phoebe to shade the bedside light and declared herself ready for sleep. 'And don't forget that I like my tea at seven o'clock,' she commanded as Phoebe bade her goodnight.

There were chores to do downstairs, but presently she locked up and went to her room where she unpacked and undressed. The room looked better already with her own things scattered round it. Tomorrow she would get some flowers and look in the cupboard on the landing and see if there was a more colourful bedspread.

Aunt Kate was asleep, looking old and frail, so that Phoebe, peeping round the door, felt a pang of real pity. With any luck, she would sleep the night through. Phoebe crept into the bathroom on the other side of the landing and turned on the old-fashioned geyser and presently sank into a hot bath. The day had been long and eventful and she was tired. It was an effort to get herself out and into her bed, and once there she was asleep at once.

She was used to getting up early. She was downstairs in the kitchen in her dressing gown making tea when Aunt Kate rang her bell. Phoebe picked up the tea tray and hurried upstairs, to find the old lady irritable and impatient.

'Still in your dressing gown?' she wanted to know. 'I hope you're not lazy . . .'

Phoebe wished her good morning, sat her up against freshly shaken pillows and offered her pills and tea. 'I'll dress while you drink your tea, and then I'll freshen you up before breakfast.'

She prudently didn't wait for Aunt Kate to disagree, but whisked herself back to her own room, got into a grey wool dress which did nothing for her at all, tied her hair back with a ribbon to save time, and went back to Aunt Kate.

Aunt Kate was as firmly against being washed and put into a clean nightie as Phoebe was determined that this was to be done. Phoebe won. A stint on Women's Medical Ward had taught her how to get round elderly ladies who wanted to do exactly the opposite of what was asked of them; calm, kindness and never-ending patience were three virtues she had acquired and she was by nature a kind girl. Aunt Kate, almost without realising it, found herself washed, clad in another of her old-fashioned nightgowns, her hair combed and pinned into a tidy knot, and then she was lifted into a bedside chair, where she sat watching clean sheets being put on her bed and wearily scolding at the extra washing which would have to be done. Phoebe popped her back into bed while she was still complaining. 'There,' she said, 'isn't that better? I'll get your breakfast.'

Coddled egg, thin bread and butter and a cup of tea, nicely arranged on a tray—even Aunt Kate could find no fault with that. Phoebe went back to the kitchen and boiled an egg, made some toast and a pot of tea and sat down at the table to eat her own breakfast, while she made a list of the shopping which had to be done. She hadn't finished when Susan arrived, accepted a cup of tea, and declared her intention of giving the kitchen a good going over. 'But I'll tidy up first, miss, only Miss Mason don't much like me in her room.'

'Then I'll do it—you see to the rest of the house, Susan, just as you always do. Dr Pritchard doesn't come until after surgery, does he? I'll go out as soon as I've seen to my aunt and do the shopping.'

Aunt Kate had eaten most of her breakfast. 'And what do you fancy for your lunch?' enquired Phoebe. 'I'm going to the shops presently. What about a morsel of chicken and potato with some mashed parsnips?'

'Chicken costs a lot of money,' observed Miss Mason.

'Cheaper than meat, Aunt Kate. And I'll get a marrow bone and make soup—that's nice with toast for supper.' She added carefully: 'I'll need some money.'

Aunt Kate put her hand under the bedclothes

and withdrew a purse; she had sat with it in her hand while Phoebe had made the bed. 'I'm a poor old woman,' she said with mournful mendacity. 'We'll be starving at this rate.'

'I'm a good manager,' Phoebe assured her, 'but there really is nothing in the larder, and you need good nourishing food. The milkman called just now and said you only had a pint every other day; I asked him to leave a pint each day. I can make milk puddings and custards which won't cost much and will do you good.' She added cunningly: 'There's masses of rice in the kitchen cupboard, and semolina too—no need to buy those for weeks.'

'You'll use up everything there is,' demanded Aunt Kate, 'and not waste my money!'

Phoebe was nipping round the room with a duster; she could have written her name on the old-fashioned mantlepiece. Obviously the nurse had either not bothered, or Aunt Kate had refused to let her keep the room clean, let alone tidy. The floor could do with a good Hoovering, only she doubted if Aunt Kate had such a thing in the house. Oblivious to her aunt's complaining voice, she wiped down the ledges and the table tops, and collected newspapers, pacifying her aunt with the paper which had just arrived. Promising to be back to give her her elevenses, she got a jacket and let herself out of the house. It was only just after nine o'clock and the street was quiet, although there were several cars outside the doctor's house. Phoebe walked the short distance to where the shops were—the butcher's, the general store and Post Office, and tucked in between these, a bow-fronted window full of small antiques. She paused a moment to peer at these before opening the door of the stores. There was no one in the shop, but the old-fashioned bell at the door brought a small round woman from the door behind the counter.

'Miss Mason's niece,' she said with satisfaction. 'Susan said you was come.'

Phoebe offered a hand over the counter. 'Phoebe Creswell,' she said politely.

'Mrs Platt. Come to stock up a bit, 'ave you? By all accounts there weren't much in the house. Can't say I blame that nurse—not that I liked her, mind you—a stuck-up piece if ever there was one.'

She studied Phoebe's pleasant not quite pretty face and nodded. 'Now what's it to be?'

Phoebe studied her list. She had whittled it down as far as she dared, for Aunt Kate hadn't been over-generous with the housekeeping. Luckily Mrs Platt was sympathetic; Phoebe made her purchases, bought some stamps for herself and went to the butcher next door. He obliged with a piece of chicken, a large bone and two lamb chops, made the observation that it was a pleasure to have her for a customer, and bade her a cheerful good morning. At least the people were friendly, she thought, and the morning was bright and the sky blue. Life could be far worse. Just for the moment she allowed her thoughts to dwell upon Basil, but only for a moment; he wasn't worth wasting time over. She went back into the house, watched, if she did but know it, by Dr Pritchard, pausing between patients. Only when she had closed the door behind her did he press his buzzer and turn an impersonally friendly face to his next patient.

Phoebe put away her purchases, made a neat list of what she had spent, and took it upstairs with her aunt's egg and milk. She listened to Aunt Kate's tirade over the cost of everything without rancour, handed over the change and observed that she was going to find out from Susan where she could buy vegetables. She slipped away before her aunt could argue.

Susan was a mine of information. Her own dad had a tidy bit of garden, she could bring anything within reason any time she was asked, she said.

So Phoebe made another list, argued prices with Susan and went back upstairs to ask for the money. 'Far cheaper than I could buy in a shop,' she pointed out cheerfully, 'and Susan will bring just as much as we need; there won't be any waste.' And this argument appealed to Aunt Kate, who produced the purse once more.

Susan had done her best with the kitchen. Phoebe shared the Nescafé with her, and, left alone, began on the lunch. She was peeling potatoes when Dr Pritchard came in. His 'Hullo,' was brisk and friendly. 'I never knock,' he advised her. 'Susan's always sweeping and dusting and I know my way around.' He gave her a quick look. 'Sleep well?'

'Me? Oh yes, thank you. Aunt Kate had a good night, she's got a very rapid pulse and a bit of a temperature; I've written them down upstairs. She ate most of her breakfast and took her pills.'

'Then we'll have a look at her, shall we?'

He waited while she washed her hands and then followed her upstairs.

Aunt Kate received him with a testy observation that she didn't need him, that she was feeling better and that if she wanted him to visit she would send a message.

To all of which he merely nodded his handsome head, observed that it was nice to see her looking so much better and that he would take a look at her chest now that he was there.

He was kind and gentle, waiting patiently while

she coughed and grumbled, struggling for breath. He put his stethoscope away presently and sat down by the bed to enquire in a leisurely fashion just how she felt.

The old lady cast him a waspish look. 'None the better for seeing you, young man. I doubt you know anything about me—all I need is a bottle of tonic to get me on my feet and something to ease the cough.'

It was no good talking to Aunt Kate about antibiotics, Phoebe could see that, and Dr Pritchard didn't really try, he remarked that it was early days for a tonic to be of much use but that he would send over a bottle of something to help the cough.

Phoebe's eyes flew to the bottles already arranged tidily on the chest of drawers, some only half finished. She looked away and caught the doctor's eye, a limpid stare which forbade her to make any comments about the half-empty bottles. It was as they went downstairs and she was on the point of opening the door for him that he said: 'Your aunt forgets easily. Pop over to the surgery in about half an hour, I'll give you a bottle of linctus; keep on with the antibiotics. Her heart's weaker, but there's nothing much I can do for congestive heart failure at this stage.'

'I'll take care of her,' said Phoebe. 'You'll—you'll come if I'm worried? There's no phone . . .'

'I'll come.' He nodded and strode off across the green. Perhaps she should have offered him a cup of coffee, she thought, watching his broad back disappearing into his house.

Life settled itself into a routine, taking care of an increasingly querulous Aunt Kate, shopping as frugally as she was able and taking snatches of time off whenever she could. The highlight of her day was Dr Pritchard's visit—not that he wasted much time on her, merely giving her fresh instructions, enquiring casually as to her own welfare and urging her to get out into the fresh air as often as she could. 'Make a point of going for a walk before you do the shopping,' he suggested. 'Susan's in the house and she'll let me know if I'm needed in a hurry.'

His intent eyes studied her face. 'You're too thin and far too pale.' He grinned suddenly.'Pining for the bright lights or a boy-friend?'

She was furious to find herself blushing. 'No, I'm very happy here.'

His grunt was unbelieving.

Days became weeks and March became April, and the early mornings were now a delight. She read letters from her friends at St Coram's and found herself glad that she wasn't there any more. There was nothing to do in Woolpit, and yet she was content with her dull life, nor did she look ahead. It was soothing to live from day to day, forgetting the past and paying no attention to the future. Aunt Kate took up more and more of her time, for she was becoming weaker and more difficult to nurse. She had no appetite now and Phoebe spent a long time with her nose in a cookery book, turning out appetising little meals which, as often as not, were not eaten. But ill though she was, Aunt Kate's tongue hadn't lost its sharpness, nothing was right. Phoebe spent too much money on the food, didn't answer the bell as quickly as she should, left her poor old aunt alone for hours on end . . .

She said nothing, because it was clear that Aunt Kate was getting worse. Dr Pritchard had taken to calling in twice a day now, never stopping for more than a few minutes, but it was

comforting to know that he was very aware of the
situation. Phoebe had been in Woolpit almost
three weeks when Aunt Kate began to go downhill
fast. Phoebe took to sitting up late and getting up
very early and then, finally, getting into her
dressing gown and sitting in a chair in Aunt Kate's
room and dozing through the night, waking at the
first cough or movement.

'Getting tired?' Dr Pritchard wanted to know.
'Hang on if you can—I don't want to upset her by
bringing in a strange face. I'll come over about
midnight. Would you like Mrs Thirsk to sleep
here?'

Phoebe shook her head. 'No, thank you all the
same. I'll be all right. If—if I'm worried I shall run
over and fetch you?'

'Right, do that.'

Her aunt was weaker when he came that
afternoon. 'Plenty to drink if she'll take it, and
keep her comfortable,' he said and went again.

With the evening the house seemed very quiet.
Phoebe saw to her patient, made herself some tea
and finally got ready for bed. She longed to sleep,
but although Aunt Kate was sleeping she looked
much worse. She curled up in a chair just beyond
the lamp's dim light and longed for Dr Pritchard
to come. But that wouldn't be for another couple
of hours.

He came long before then, opening the street
door and calling softly as he came into the house.
When he came into the room Phoebe got out of
the chair. 'I am glad you're here,' she whispered. 'I
don't think—that is, I think Aunt Kate's not so
well . . .'

He had gone to bend over his patient. 'We won't
disturb her. I'll stay—you can go to bed, you're
asleep on your feet!'

'Is she . . .?' And when he nodded: 'I'll stay, she's my aunt.'

So they sat facing each other in the big bedroom while Aunt Kate slipped peacefully away. It was after midnight when the doctor stood up finally.

'You'd better sleep at my place,' he suggested gently.

'I'll be quite all right, thank you. Would you like tea before you go?'

'A good idea. I'll get the writing done while you are making it. You'd rather stay here?'

'Yes.' She went past him and down to the kitchen and put the kettle on. There was really a good deal to think about, but she was far too tired.

They drank their tea almost in silence, while Dr Pritchard did his writing, and she got up and went to the door with him when he'd finished. It was a chilly night and she shivered as she opened it, and not altogether with cold, although her thanks and goodnight were composed enough. He took the door handle from her. 'Mrs Thirsk will be over in five minutes,' he told her and was gone before she could argue.

Indeed, she didn't much want to argue. She was thankful not to be alone in the house despite her assurances to him, and the housekeeper's matter-of-fact presence was comforting. She waved away Phoebe's apologies, took the cup of tea which she was offered and sat talking about nothing much for a few minutes. Then she got up briskly, asked where the hot water bottles were kept, filled them, gave one to Phoebe and told her with brisk kindness to go to bed. 'And no getting up at crack of dawn,' she warned. 'I'll see that you're up in time for Susan before I get the doctor's breakfast.'

Phoebe hardly heard her. She said goodnight in a wispy voice and went upstairs and presently got into her bed, listening with childish relief to Mrs Thirsk's rather heavy footfall mounting to the room on the other side of the landing. The bed hadn't been made up, thought Phoebe sleepily, and closed her eyes.

When she opened them Mrs Thirsk was standing by the bed with a cup of tea in her hand. 'Plenty of time, Phoebe. Just you drink this up and then come down when you're ready. I've put everything out for your breakfast. I'll be off now—you'll be all right?'

Phoebe sat up in bed, her mousy hair a fine curtain round her still pale face. 'Oh, Mrs Thirsk, thank you! Yes, of course I will.' She hesitated. 'I'm not sure what to do ...'

'Doctor will be over when he's had his breakfast—he'll know,' said Mrs Thirsk comfortably.

Things seemed so different now. The morning was bright and sunny and Dr Pritchard would see to everything. Phoebe dressed and got her breakfast, then opened the door to Susan, who in some mysterious way knew all about Aunt Kate. 'Poor ol' soul,' she observed in her soft courteous country voice. 'She'll be better off where she is. When's the funeral, miss?'

Phoebe shook her head. 'I don't know—I don't know anything at present.'

Dr Pritchard came then, and sat himself down at the kitchen table. 'The district nurse will be here in a few minutes,' he observed. 'Now listen to me ...'

He had thought of everything. When he had finished he said, 'Mr Cole, your aunt's solicitor, will come here for the funeral—you'll stay here for the time being, of course. Do you mind being in the house alone?'

'No.' She glanced at Susan, sitting between them, listening to every word. 'Susan and I could springclean.'

'You'll sleep here on your own?'

'Oh, yes.' She looked enquiringly at him and he said: 'You'll have it to yourself, Phoebe.' He started for the door. 'Borrow Mrs Thirk's bike and take yourself off for a ride round, and don't come back until after twelve.' He smiled. 'Doctor's orders!'

The next day or so went quickly enough. Susan came each morning and the pair of them scrubbed and polished and turned out cupboards and drawers, and Phoebe was too tired in the evenings to do more than tumble into bed. She saw almost nothing of Dr Pritchard, but he was there, on the other side of the green, and she was content with that.

It surprised her that so many people came to the funeral. The church was full, but only a handful of people came back to the house afterwards and they didn't stay long. And when the last one had gone Mr Cole sat down in the sitting room and opened his briefcase.

'Miss Mason's will is brief,' he began in his dry elderly voice. 'It was made some months ago, before you came to nurse your aunt.' He smoothed the paper in his hand. 'I will read it to you.'

Aunt Kate had left every penny she possessed, a not inconsiderable amount, to charity, and the house was to be sold and the proceeds of it given to a list of charities she named. 'I leave nothing to my sole surviving relation, Phoebe Creswell,' she had written. 'She is young and strong enough to make her own way in life.'

Mr Cole coughed and folded the paper carefully. 'I regret this, Miss Creswell—you could, of course, contest it.'

Phoebe shook her head. She supposed that in the back of her mind she had nurtured the faint hope that Aunt Kate had left her a small sum, but she wasn't surprised at the will and since Aunt Kate didn't want her to have any money, then she for her part had no intention of trying to get it.

'I can go back to nursing,' she pointed out quite cheerfully, 'and I really didn't expect anything, Mr Cole. Aunt Kate didn't like me—indeed, we hardly knew each other.'

Mr Cole grunted morosely. 'I still regret it, my dear. You have, after all, interrupted your training in order to look after her.'

'Yes, but I daresay she didn't realise that. I can always start again.'

'There is, of course, no hurry for you to leave here. The place will have to be sold, but it will probably take some time and it will be all the better for someone living here. Have you any money?'

'Well, I can manage for a week or two, but I can't afford to pay Susan.'

Mr Cole looked thoughtful. 'Ah yes—well ... it would be quite in order for the estate to settle her wages until such time as the house is sold. I can arrange that and I will see that she is told. You will remain for the time being?' Phoebe said yes, she would. A week or two would give her time to apply to be taken on as a student nurse—not in London, though. She didn't want to go back there, she didn't much care if she never saw London again, nor St Coram's, nor Basil. Certainly not Basil.

He arrived the next day, driving up in his flashy little car and hooting furiously in front of the house. Phoebe, upstairs sorting blankets, poked her head out of the window, and when she saw who it was, gazed down at him speechlessly.

'Hullo there—aren't you going to let me in?' He spoke loudly enough for the neighbours to hear— indeed, Dr Pritchard, on the other side of the green, heard him and turned a placid gaze on him through his surgery window. He had been about to ring for the next patient, now he took his hand off the bell and waited to see what would happen.

Phoebe withdrew her head and went down to open the door, to stand squarely in the doorway. She didn't invite Basil in. Not only was she aware that several people would be peering through their windows at her, but she really didn't want to see Basil. She realised this with great relief. She had got over him entirely—indeed, looking at him, she wondered how on earth she could ever have thought she was in love with him in the first place.

She said soberly, 'Hullo, Basil,' and waited.

'Well, aren't I to come in?' he asked, and flashed her his charming smile.

'No, I'd rather you didn't.'

He shrugged. 'I've driven all this way to see how you were getting on. How's that aunt of yours?'

'Aunt Kate died a few days ago.'

'Left you all her wordly goods and the house? Lucky you!'

'Aunt Kate didn't leave me anything.'

'The miserable old . . .' He stopped at the look on Phoebe's face.

'She was my aunt, she was entitled to leave her money to anyone she wished. I hardly knew her.'

'Hard luck, old girl. Coming back to St Coram's?'

Phoebe studied his face. Very good-looking, but there was something missing. 'No.'

'Oh, come on, now!'

'Why do you ask?'

He shrugged again. He wasn't going to tell her that he had had a bet with some of the other housemen that he would persuade her to return to St Coram's. 'Idle curiosity. I say, aren't you really going to ask me in?'

'No.' She added: 'I'm very busy. Goodbye.' She closed the door in his face.

Basil muttered to himself, got into his car and roared off, and Dr Pritchard, his face still placid, rang for the next patient.

When he had done his morning rounds he crossed the green and knocked on the door. Phoebe, still upstairs, poked her head out of the window again. She said with marked relief: 'Oh, it's you—I'll come down. Susan's just gone.'

She was very untidy and faintly grubby with it. Dr Pritchard eyed her keenly and went past her into the kitchen. 'Having a busy morning?' he wanted to know.'

'Well, yes, there is a lot to do. The whole house needs a good clean, and I'm making an inventory—in case someone wants to buy the furniture and things.'

'Not lonely?'

'No, Susan comes.'

'Your aunt didn't leave you the house?' The doctor sounded very casual.

Phoebe hadn't told anyone about the will. 'No—she left everything, this house as well, to charities. I'm just staying for a few days. Mr Cole said I could until they put the house up for sale, it'll give me a chance to apply for training somewhere.'

He leaned against the kitchen table. 'And that's what you intend to do?'

'Yes,' said Phoebe in a determined voice. She picked up the crockery spread on the table, ready to pack, and started to stack it neatly.

'Start all over again?'

'I'll have to, won't I?'

'Only if that's what you want.' He went to the door. 'You and I must have a talk. A pity I have to go out this evening. How about tomorrow morning? Before surgery? Say eight o'clock, we'll have half an hour. I've been having breakfast at half-past seven—have it with me?'

She hesitated. 'Thank you, but isn't that—I mean, isn't it rather an odd time?'

He grinned. 'I don't imagine anyone in the village could possibly weave a romance round breakfast at half-past seven in the morning, do you?'

Phoebe went pink. 'No, of course not. Aren't I silly ... I'd like to come. What do you want to talk about?'

He was suddenly serious. 'Why, your future, Phoebe, what else?'

She went back to her sorting of the contents of the linen cupboard, wondering why he should show even a faint interest in what she intended to do. But it spurred her on to make some definite plans. When she had finished with the endless counterpanes, pillowcases and enormous linen sheets her aunt had favoured, she changed into the grey dress, did her face and tidied her hair and went down to Mrs Platt's shop. One end of the counter was stacked with weekly magazines and daily newspapers, but there wasn't a *Nursing Mirror* or *Nursing Times* among them. Phoebe bought some sausages for her supper, then crossed the street to the row of brick cottages where the district nurse lived. Nurse Wilkins was at home, getting her lunch and feeding her cats; she called 'Come in' in answer to Phoebe's knock and shouted: 'I'm in the kitchen, come through.' She smiled when she saw who it was, 'Hullo, love, feeling lonely?'

Phoebe shook her head. 'I've got too much to do—the house goes up for sale in a few days and I'm getting it ready.'

'Miss Mason didn't leave it to you? The village seemed to think she might, and she had pots of money.'

'Everything is to go to several charities.' And at the look of disbelief on her companion's face: 'It doesn't matter—I hadn't expected anything, she didn't have anything to do with the family for years and years.'

'Until she needed someone to nurse her. What are you going to do?'

'That's why I came. Have you any copies of the *Nursing Times*? I'll apply to start training.'

'But didn't I hear that you'd done a year already? Won't your old hospital take you back?'

'I don't want to go back to London. I'd forgotten how lovely it is living in the country. I thought I'd try a provincial town.'

Nurse Wilkins prudently refrained from pointing out that the country could be quite a long way from a provincial town large enough to have a training school for nurses. 'You'll find a pile in the sitting room—there are some *Nursing Mirrors* there too—take as many as you want. I'd ask you to stay to have a meal, but I popped back for half an hour from a midder case. I'm sorry you've had such rotten luck.'

'That's all right. Actually I've liked being here very much, and thanks.'

Nurse Wilkins waved her spoon at her. 'Any time.'

There were depressingly few hospitals offering vacancies. Phoebe made a careful note of them

while she ate her lunch and then sat down to apply
to each one of them. She couldn't expect to be
taken on for at least a month, but she had a little
money saved, so perhaps she could find a job in
Stowmarket while she waited for the answers.
She wrote her letters, and since she had no
stamps and Mrs Platt was closed for the half
day, put on her jacket and took herself off for a
long walk. The house seemed very empty when
she got back. She made tea, then sat in the
kitchen at the table and worked out how long
she would be able to manage on the money she
had. The result wasn't very satisfactory. She
went into the sitting room and settled down to
washing the china in the cabinet opposite the
window. While she was doing it she saw Dr
Pritchard, splendid in a black tie, get into his
Bristol and drive off. Somehow the sight of him
made her feel lonelier than ever. She ate her
sausages gloomily, then took herself off to bed
and stayed awake a long time feeling depressed.

It was a relief to wake early to a lovely morning
with the sun already streaming through the
window. She got up and dressed in the grey dress
once more, did her hair rather more severely than
usual and at half-past seven crossed the green and
rang Dr Pritchard's bell.

Mrs Thirsk opened the door with a cheerful
good morning, and the news that she was on the
point of dishing up the bacon and eggs and would
Phoebe like to go straight into the dining room.
'Doctor had an early morning call, and he's having
a shave, but he'll be down in a moment.'

'Oh,' said Phoebe, 'perhaps some other time—I
mean, I daresay he's tired . . .'

'No, he's not, only ravenous. Good morning,
Phoebe.' He had come down the stairs and caught

her arm and whisked her into the dining room. 'Pour the coffee, there's a good girl.'

She did as she was asked, taking a quick look at him. He didn't look in the least tired and his manner was as unhurried as it always was.

Mrs Thirsk came in with their breakfast then, and beyond a word here and there for politeness' sake, he said very little. Only when they had got to the toast and marmalade and his third cup of coffee did he ask: 'Made any plans?'

'I've borrowed some nursing magazines from Nurse Wilkins and written to five hospitals to see if they'll take me in their training schools.'

'Posted them?'

Phoebe thought it a funny question. 'As a matter of fact, no—I hadn't any stamps.'

'Good. Tear them up, I've got a much better idea.'

She opened her grey eyes wide. 'You have? Whatever is it?'

'It seems to me to be an excellent idea if we were to get married.'

Phoebe's eyes almost popped out of her head. 'Married? You and me? But you don't and I don't ... that is, we don't know anything about each other.'

'Oh, I know a great deal about you, quite enough to be sure you'll make me an excellent wife. As for me—well, I live here, don't I? I live in this house and intend to live here for the rest of my life. I like it here. I like to travel too. My mother is Dutch; my father died several years ago and she spends a good deal of the year in Holland—she has a home there as well as a house in Grantchester; naturally I visit her frequently.'

Phoebe closed her open mouth to ask: 'You're half Dutch?' A silly question, but it was all she could think of.

'Yes.' He smiled at her. 'I could practise there if I wished—I qualified there as well as in England.'

'Oh, yes, well . . .' She gave him a bewildered stare. 'But why do you want to marry me?'

I'm thirty-two and it's time I settled down. I haven't met a girl I wanted to marry, someone who would fit into my life—but you, you would. We could, of course, get to know each other better, have a long engagement, but what would be the point of that? You have no plans for the future, no money, no family, your heart is whole . . .'

Phoebe nodded. 'Yes, oh yes. But I'm not sure . . . I mean, would it work?'

'I can't think why not. We get on well, don't we? We might just as well get married now and get to know each other.' He smiled kindly. 'I won't rush you, Phoebe. We'll have a month or two of getting to know each other, just as an engaged couple would, only we'll get married for the sake of convenience.'

Phoebe was still bowled over. 'I—I must think about it—it's a bit of a surprise.'

He glanced at his watch and said matter-of-factly: 'Off you go, then. I must start surgery. Only promise me one thing—don't send those letters until you've made up your mind. Give it a couple of days' thought.'

'All right,' said Phoebe, 'I'll think about it, and I won't send those letters.'

'Good girl! I must fly.' He patted her shoulder and left the room as Mrs Thirsk came in.

'It was a lovely breakfast,' said Phoebe. 'Thank you, Mrs Thirsk.' She had no idea how agitated her face looked, nor did she see Mrs Thirsk's thoughtful glance. 'I must get on with the packing up,' she told that lady, and got herself out of the house.

'That's a right old shame that Miss Mason left all that money to silly old charities,' Susan greeted her. News spread fast in the village.

'Charities do a lot of good,' said Phoebe feebly. 'I wonder if the house is put up for sale yet?' She put a hand to her head. She must forget about Dr Pritchard for the moment, there was still a lot to do. Later she would sit down quietly and decide what was best. It would have helped a lot if there had been someone in whom she could have confided.

CHAPTER THREE

IT disconcerted Phoebe very much not to see anything of Dr Pritchard for the next two days. For once quite unable to make up her sensible mind, she fought the urge to go across the green and bang on his door—an urge she suppressed until the evening of the second day. Then she suddenly flung down the curtains she was folding away into the landing cupboard, opened the street door and hurried across the green to beat a tattoo on his knocker.

Mrs Thirsk opened the door, bade her enter and said comfortably: 'You'll be wanting to see the doctor? He's gone to Baxter's farm to see their youngest—measles, by all accounts. He'll be back in about ten minutes. Come in and sit down.'

Phoebe sidled to the door. 'No—no, thanks. It was just something . . . not important—any time will do.' She actually had her hand on the doorknob when Mrs Thirsk said matter-of-factly: 'Seeing as you're here, it makes sense to stay, otherwise he'll go across to see you when he could just as soon be sitting cosy by his own hearth.' She smiled suddenly and opened the sitting room door. 'He won't be above a few minutes.'

So Phoebe went and sat down in the smaller of the armchairs on either side of the hearth, and Beauty came and sat with her, pressed up against her legs, yawning into the log fire. It was a pleasant room and peaceful, and somehow knowing that she was there sent her problems oozing away. She had been a fool to come in the first place, she decided. How did one seek advice about marrying someone when that someone was the person expected to give the advice?

The knotty point was settled for her by the doctor's quiet entry.

'You look quite at home sitting there, Phoebe.' He smiled at her and sat down in the big wing chair opposite her, and Beauty moved across to lay her head on his shoes. 'What's the trouble?' He shot her a keen look. 'Or is it just the pleasure of my company?'

'I like being with you,' said Phoebe ingenuously, and didn't see the gleam in his eyes. 'It's a bit difficult—you see, I want to talk to someone and ask their advice, only there isn't anyone—only you, and you're the person I want advice about.'

'I'll do my best to be impartial,' he told her gravely.

'Oh, good. It's like this . . .' She paused and asked hurriedly: 'Have you had your supper—am I keeping you from that? Or—or reading or anything?'

'Supper's an hour or more away, but we'll have a drink while we're talking.' He got up and poured her a glass of sherry and gave himself a whisky, then settled back comfortably in his chair.

Phoebe took a sip of sherry and then another one. 'Did you really mean that you wanted to marry me?'

'Yes, I meant it.'

'Do you think we would be happy? I mean, just being friends without being in love and all that?'

The corners of his firm mouth twitched. 'Yes, being friends is very important if you're married—you can love someone, or be in love with someone, and dislike them intensely.'

She nodded, thinking fleetingly of Basil. 'Yes,

but suppose you fell in love with someone after we were married?'

'Or you fell in love, Phoebe, or someone fell in love with you?'

She shook her head. 'I don't think that's very likely. I'm not pretty, you must have noticed . . .'

'I can't say I had.' His voice was gentle. 'And as for me, I've had years in which to fall in love and marry, haven't I? I've fancied myself in love on countless occasions—you too, I daresay.'

She didn't answer him because it wasn't a question. 'You don't think that if I married you, I'd be doing it because it was easier than looking for a job?'

The doctor was taken with a fit of coughing. 'Er—no, the thought hadn't crossed my mind.'

'You really think it would work?'

'Indeed I do—but we'll make haste slowly, don't you agree? Get to know each other for a month or so.'

'You mean after we're married?'

'Yes. I'm quite sure that, given time, we shall become a happily married couple.'

Phoebe's grey eyes looked into the future. She liked him very much; she would miss him if she were never to see him again. He was a comfortable companion, and she, so shy and uncertain with people she met, had always felt as if she was at ease with him. She said slowly: 'If you're quite sure, I'd like to marry you. Will you let me share your life, though? I wouldn't want to stay at home all day—and you've got Mrs Thirsk. She might not like it . . .'

The doctor bent to stroke Beauty's head. 'Mrs Thirsk is my housekeeper, Phoebe, and will continue to be that, but you will run my home— she'll gladly show you how to set about it—and of course you'll share my life; help in the surgery if you like, answer letters ... besides, I have a number of friends, and I hope they'll be your friends too.'

'I'm not much good at meeting people,' said Phoebe doubtfully.

'I think you'll find they'll be very easy to get on with.' He became brisk all of a sudden. 'Have you any family or friends you'd want to come to the wedding?'

'I haven't any family at all now, and no close friends at St Coram's.'

'Then we'll have a very quiet wedding here, shall we? Just a couple of witnesses and Mrs Thirsk. Quite early in the day, don't you think? I've a week or so holiday due, we'll go to Holland and you can meet my family.'

He thought for a minute. 'When is Miss Mason's house being put on the market?'

'Tomorrow.'

'Well, no one is likely to buy it at once, and if they do it will be a week or two before they can possibly move in. You can stay there until I can make arrangements for us to marry. We won't bother with the banns—I'll get a licence, you'll want to do some shopping, I expect. I'll drive you to Cambridge—I've got a half day on Friday. Have you any money?'

Phoebe did a few sums in her head. 'Enough to buy a new suit or something.'

He nodded. 'Good. You're quite happy about this, Phoebe?'

Strangely enough, despite their businesslike conversation, she was. It would need a bit of getting used to, of course, but it was lovely to feel that someone wanted her and didn't seem to mind that she wasn't stunningly pretty. It seemed

strange that George—she must really think of him
as George—with his good looks and placid charm,
hadn't wanted to marry a really stunning girl. Of
course, clothes would help, and a new hairstyle
and make-up . . .

'Hey, come back,' said George softly. 'You're a
long way away.'

She smiled at him. 'I was wondering why you'd
picked on me—I mean, there must be dozens of
girls . . .'

'Dozens,' he agreed placidly, 'but I haven't
fancied any of them.' He grinned. 'Perhaps I'm not
romantic.'

She had no chance to answer him, because Mrs
Thirsk tapped softly on the door and put her head
round it to ask: 'Will Miss Creswell be staying for
supper, Doctor? There's a nice steak and kidney
pie . . .'

'Indeed she will, Mrs Thirsk, and we'd like you
to be the first to know that Miss Creswell and I
are going to get married.'

Mrs Thirsk came right into the room, beaming.
'Well, I never did! If that isn't as good a piece of
news as I've heard for I don't know how long!' She
shook hands with them both. 'And won't the
village be pleased! Took to you, they have,' she
explained to Phoebe, 'just the wife for the doctor.
When's it to be?'

'As soon as I can arrange it. And very quiet, Mrs
Thirsk, just us and two witnesses and yourself.'

'I must get a new hat,' declared Mrs Thirsk,
and marched off to the kitchen, humming the
Wedding March in a surprisingly tuneful voice.

The doctor laughed gently. 'And will you have a
new hat, Phoebe?'

She said seriously: 'Oh, yes, I think so, I mean,
it's a wedding.'

He got up. 'Let's have supper,' and when she got up too, he took her hands and kissed her on the cheek. 'We shall be happy, Phoebe, you and I.'

She felt happy and content. Probably, she thought, she would wake in the small hours and panic, but there was no need for that. George wasn't the kind of man one panicked about; they would lead a pleasant life together, growing closer as the years went by and they got to know each other. She would enjoy being a doctor's wife and she wished for nothing better than to live in Woolpit for the rest of her life. It would take time to adjust, of course, but he had said he wouldn't hurry her. She would, she promised herself silently, be a good wife.

They ate their supper together, talking like old friends. She told him about her childhood, not realising how bleak it sounded; she told him about Basil too. 'Of course, it was silly of me,' she observed, 'only I was so pleased that he'd noticed me—I thought he really liked me, but of course he was only amusing himself.'

'You're sure of that?' The question was asked casually.

'Yes, perhaps when I first came here I hoped . . . but when he came the other day I knew at once that I never wanted to see him again.' She smiled across the table. 'Isn't it funny how one discovers quite suddenly that something—someone—that one thought mattered doesn't mean a thing?'

'And that acts the other way too—something that means nothing at all is suddenly all-important.'

They sat for a while talking after supper before Phoebe said it was high time that she went back. She felt faint disappointment when George made

no effort to keep her, a disappointment mitigated
to some extent by the kiss he gave her when they
reached her doorstep. She hadn't much experience
of being kissed; she'd enjoyed this one, although
thinking about it afterwards she felt vaguely
disquieted. George had kissed her with warmth
rather like an old friend, but not, she considered,
as a man who was about to marry her. But why
should she expect more? she argued as she
undressed. They were only friends, after all, he had
never once mentioned being in love with her—but
then he wasn't was he? Basil had kissed her several
times and called her darling and declared that she
was a wonderful girl, but he hadn't meant a word
of it. George, she felt sure, would only say things
like that if he meant them. She sighed a little
wistfully and fell asleep.

The postman came while she was getting her
breakfast. She had overslept and hadn't hurried
over her dressing, and it was almost nine o'clock.
The house agents were sending Mr and Mrs James
over in half an hour to view the house and would
she be good enough to show them round? She had
planned a walk, but instead she gobbled her
breakfast, made her bed and tidied the already
spotless house, and was waiting in her grey dress
again to open the door when a large Mercedes
drew up before it.

A thin, sharp-faced man got out first, followed
by a tall stout woman who overshadowed him
completely. It was she who rapped on the door
knocker and answered Phoebe's polite 'Good
morning' with a condescending nod, and an
impatient: 'Well, come in, Arthur!'

They went slowly round the house, making
disparaging remarks about the worn curtains, the
rather nice furniture Phoebe had so carefully

polished and the old-fashioned wallpaper. Susan was in the kitchen, cleaning the sink, and the woman paused to stare at her. 'Who's she?' she asked.

'This is Susan, she lives in the village and comes here every morning.'

Mrs James sniffed. 'I'll engage my own servant,' she observed, and ran a finger along one of the shelves and examined it for dust.

They went at last, and Phoebe made coffee for Susan and herself. 'Let's hope they don't buy the house,' she said. 'I don't think they'd be very happy in the village.'

'Not likely, they wouldn't, miss.' But Susan didn't waste time on the Jameses; she wanted to talk about the wedding. In some mysterious way she had known about Phoebe and Dr Pritchard getting engaged, and she assured Phoebe that the whole village knew anyway. 'And we're all that pleased,' she told her. 'What will you wear?'

More people came in the afternoon, pleasant elderly couples who said very little and went away without expressing any wish to buy the house. Phoebe had her tea rather late and when she was at last free to do so went for a walk. She hadn't seen George to speak to; he had gone off in his car in the morning, and although she had seen him getting into it again after lunch, he hadn't as much as looked her way. She walked back briskly, deciding what she would cook for her supper, and met George on her doorstep.

'Hullo,' he greeted her with his usual placid friendliness. 'Surgery's finished and I've only got a couple of calls to make, so come over when you're ready and wait for me.'

'Yes, all right—I was just going to get my supper . . .'

'Whatever for? You'll have supper with me each

evening—it's about the only time we'll get to talk.'
He patted her on the shoulder with a large hand
and went back across the green, then got into his
car and drove away.

Phoebe changed the grey dress for a brown one,
almost as dull. In a day or two, she told herself
happily, she would go shopping. She had written
to the bank and asked them to transfer her
account to Stowmarket. Provided the house agents
left her in peace she could catch the bus there one
morning and draw out most of her savings. She
had always bought her clothes with an eye to their
durability, but now she would let herself go . . .

Mrs Thirsk opened the door to her, led her to
the sitting room and informed her with satisfaction
that the village, to a man, were delighted to hear
that she and the doctor were to marry. Having
said which, she took herself off to the kitchen,
leaving Phoebe to sit and sniff appreciatively at the
fragrant smells coming from it.

The doctor arrived presently, with Beauty at his
heels.

'Oh, I wondered where she was,' said Phoebe.
'Does she go with you on your rounds?'

'If I haven't many visits, yes. Have you had
anyone to look at the house?'

She told him while they had their drinks. 'Well,
you can't sit around all day,' he observed. 'I'll
phone the agents in the morning and tell them to
send people either morning or afternoon—which
suits you best?'

'Afternoon, I think. Would they mind?'

He looked surprised. 'Perhaps, but if you
weren't there they would have to send a clerk each
time, you know.'

Phoebe didn't argue; it was wonderful to have
someone who bothered about her. They spent the

rest of the evening planning their wedding, and although George's kiss was exactly the same as the last one—an old friend's—she had found it somehow very comforting. The more she saw of him the more she was sure they would be happy together—no high-flown romance, perhaps, but genuine regard for each other.

She went for a walk in the morning, shopped for her lunch and sat down to wait for any possible viewers. An elderly couple came first. She found them pleasant because they didn't make remarks about anything. The second couple found fault with everything, told her that she hadn't a hope of selling a dump that had no central heating, no double glazing and no plumbing for a washing machine. They called it plain speaking, but she found them downright rude. She made tea after they had gone; it was well past four o'clock and it wasn't likely that anyone else would come before five now.

She was washing the tea things when the door-knocker was thumped. She sighed and went to answer it. There was a youngish man on the doorstep, dressed in leather, his hair hanging untidily round his neck. A vast motorbike had been parked on the verge and he was taking off his helmet.

'House for sale?' he asked, and gave her a grin.

'The agents sent you?' asked Phoebe.

'Course they did. I'll have a quick dekko, love.'

He had pushed past her and was in the hall before she could answer and he had gone ahead of her into the sitting room. Phoebe, not much liking him, recited her short rigmarole about size and furniture and coal fires and all the rest of it and led him into the kitchen. He wasn't very interested; he glanced at the pantry, the scullery and the

garden from the window and asked: 'Upstairs,
love? Got a bathroom?'

She led the way, opened the doors of the
bedrooms and the bathroom and stood on the
landing while he went from one to the other. She
remembered uneasily that her aunt's silver treas-
ures were spread out on the bed in the smallest
bedroom. They were waiting to be wrapped and
packed away. She had got them out before tea and
had cleaned them and had intended to wrap them
carefully and put them in the locked cupboard in
her aunt's room. The man was there now, picking
up the silver trinket boxes, the brushes, the heavy
mirror and the small silver vases. He glanced over
his shoulder at her.

'Nice bit of stuff here—worth a bit,' he
remarked softly. 'Can't say I think much of the
house, but these will do me.'

'Put them back!' said Phoebe sharply. 'And get
out of this house!'

'Before you call the police?' He laughed nastily.
'No phone either, is there, and you'll never get to
the door, love. I'll take what I fancy and go quiet-
like and no sneaking when I've gone or I'll come
back and break your jaw!'

Phoebe could feel her knees wobbling, but rage
sent her into her bedroom to slam the door in his
face and put her head out of the window and
screech 'George!' at the top of her voice. For all
she knew he wasn't even home, but if he was and
he'd heard her, she knew he would come.

She wasn't given the chance to find out, though,
for the door behind her was flung open and the
man stood there, the nasty smile back on his face
just staring at her. And now she was frightened.
She turned her head and opened her mouth to
shout again, but he pushed past her and banged

the window shut. It gave her an opportunity to kick his shins, something she did with a kind of desperate satisfaction. The slap he gave her sent her head swinging sideways and the tears starting up to her eyes, but she got in another kick before he caught her roughly by the arm and pushed her on to the landing. 'You asked for it,' he called her a vile name and she said in a choking voice: 'Don't use that kind of language to me. Get out of the house before someone comes!' Her eyes fell on his loaded pockets. 'And put everything back on the bed.'

He leaned against the wall, just looking at her and saying nothing, and she wondered what he was going to do next. Her heart had sunk to her boots. George hadn't heard her—worse, he couldn't have been at home. The front door, she remembered, had shut behind the man as he had come in and would have locked automatically. She took a breath and gulped back her fear; someone would surely see the motorbike presently and wonder whose it was. 'What are you going to do?' she asked.

He took a hand from a pocket and showed her the flick-knife. 'See this, love? You're no beauty, but even a plain face can be made plainer . . .'

Phoebe thought she would be sick; a Victorian Miss would have swooned and at least delayed matters, but she was a remarkably healthy girl who had never fainted in her life. Her mouth was so dry that she couldn't speak, only stare back at him defiantly. At last she said in a whisper: 'You're like something nasty under a stone . . .'

He laughed loudly at that—a good thing, because he didn't hear the faint creak of the stairs as the doctor came up them two at a time. The laugh came to an abrupt halt as his chin came in contact with a huge fist and he slithered to the floor, Aunt Kate's silver falling and tumbling around him in a silvery shower.

The doctor stepped over him and plucked Phoebe from the windowsill she had been clinging to, and held her close. 'My poor girl—I came as fast as I could, but I had to go round the back and through the kitchen window. Has he hurt you?'

She lifted a pale face to his; the slap had left an angry red mark on one cheek. 'He slapped me,' she said in a shaky voice, 'but I kicked him.' She began to cry in earnest. 'Oh, George, suppose you hadn't come . . .'

'But I did come,' he said in a comforting voice, 'and I shall always come when you want me, Phoebe—don't forget that.' He bent and kissed her gently. 'Brave girl, but I think this is the end of you staying here alone. I'll get hold of Nurse Wilkins—you can stay with her.'

He bent over the man lying on the floor, still keeping an arm round her.

'Now run across and phone the police—ask them to come here.' He touched the supine man with the toe of his shoe. 'I'll stay here until they come.'

His voice, placid still, brooked no arguing, only at the door she paused. 'You'll be all right? He's got a knife—George, be careful.'

'Has he indeed.' The doctor had sat himself down on the side of the bed. He smiled faintly. 'I'll be careful.'

Phoebe raced away to bang on the door of his house, give a rapid and rather incoherent account to Mrs Thirsk and ring the police. That done, she turned to the housekeeper, standing right by her. 'Do you think the doctor will be all right?' she wanted to know urgently. 'That man might attack him ...' At which Mrs Thirsk laughed comfortably.

'I'd like to see him try—just you set your mind at ease, Miss Phoebe; Doctor'll take care of himself. Now you just come with me and I'll bathe that cheek and make you a nice cup of tea—a proper nasty shock you've had.'

Being fussed over made Phoebe feel a whole lot better. All the same, as she sat sipping her tea, she worried about George. Suppose the man attacked him? Stabbed him? She imagined him lying on the floor bleeding and could bear it no longer. She put her cup and saucer down and started for the door, to be halted by the quiet arrival of a police car.

She watched from the window—the police officer being admitted by George, their return with the man, who was put into the car with the other officer, and their unhurried approach to the doctor's front door. She had just the time to fly back to her chair by the fire and assume an expression of calm she didn't feel before they came in.

Short work was made of her statement. She answered questions in a level voice and left the doctor to discuss the outcome with the police officer. Presently he went away, and George gave her a drink, poured himself a whisky and sat down opposite her.

'Feeling better?' His voice was kind and concerned and she stopped worrying. 'That settled it—you'll not stay in that house any longer. You can sleep at Nurse Wilkins' and spend your days here. We'll collect what you need for the night, and you can pack tomorrow morning. The agents can send a man with anyone who wants to look over the place.'

He got up and came to bend over her, examining her reddened cheek. 'My poor dear, does it hurt much?'

She shook her head. 'Thank you, George—I was so frightened.'

He smiled. 'I'm not surprised, I'd like to keep you here, but I have my reputation to think of.'

Phoebe looked at him and saw that he was laughing softly now, and for no reason at all she laughed too; it was nice to feel so safe.

George went with her presently to fetch an overnight bag, going upstairs and sitting on the bed while she rummaged round collecting what she needed. 'I'll see Susan in the morning,' he told her, 'and tell her not to come any more for the moment; she'll go on being paid and probably when the house is sold, the new people will be glad to have her back. You'll move all your things out tomorrow, Phoebe. Mrs Thirsk will go with you while you do that and then the house will be locked up. I'll attend to the agents for you. They can make their own arrangements.'

To all of which Phoebe happily agreed. It was as they walked the short distance to Nurse Wilkins' cottage that George said: 'Come over to lunch tomorrow, Phoebe, we'll get the wedding fixed up and I'll let John Matthews, the vicar, know. I'm free in the afternoon, we'll do your shopping if you like.'

'I'd like that ... at least, I've still got to go to Stowmarket—my money's being transferred there, so could we go there first?'

'Waste of time—you can pay me back later. I haven't another half day until next week, and by then we'll probably be married.' He spoke so matter-of-factly that she felt no surprise. Until that moment, although they had discussed the wedding,

no dates had been suggested, and she had thought
vaguely of several weeks ahead, but now she was
glad that it was to be so soon. She said happily:
'Oh, will we? You'll be sure and tell me how much
I owe you, won't you?' She stopped suddenly.
'George, I've unsettled you such a lot since I
came—you're still sure?'

He took her hand and walked on. 'Quite sure.
Indeed, I quite like being unsettled.'

He didn't stay long at Nurse Wilkins' cottage,
only took her case up to the small bedroom at the
back of the landing, thanked Nurse Wilkins for
her kindness, dropped the lightest of kisses on
Phoebe's cheek and left.

'See you at lunch,' he said as he went.

There was no question of going to bed, because
Nurse Wilkins wanted to know just what had
happened. They sat in the tiny sitting room while
Phoebe told her over a pot of tea.

'Knocked him out, did he?' commented Nurse
Wilkins. 'Tied him up too—did the police mind?'

'I don't know. Shouldn't he have done that? The
man could have escaped . . .'

Nurse Wilkins nodded. 'He could too, and done
the same thing to some other poor soul. Lucky
Dr Pritchard heard you scream.' She poured
them both more tea. 'Now, what are you going to
wear for your wedding?'

Phoebe still had no idea about that as George
parked the car in Cambridge. She had spent a
dreamless night, packed her things in Mrs Thirsk's
friendly company, and then had lunch with
George. She had been accepted into his household
without fuss, indeed she was beginning to feel she
had known George for years, so relaxed was he in
her company. Which was, she told herself, entirely
satisfactory, although right at the back of her

mind there was the unwelcome thought that it
would have been even more satisfactory if he had
displayed more interest in her as a person. It
seemed to her that he accepted her as an old friend
of many years' standing, nice to have around but
incapable of exciting him in any way. He took her
arm now. 'Wedding clothes first? There are some
good boutiques . . .'

They strolled along, looking in shop windows,
until he came to a halt outside a small elegant
shop window. 'That's it,' he said. 'Do you suppose
it'll fit?' He measured her with his eye. 'You're
rather small and too thin.'

Phoebe studied the outfit in the window; a fine
wool crêpe in a deep honey colour, a pleated skirt,
straight jacket and a patterned silky top.

'It'll cost too much,' she suggested soberly, 'and
I've got quite a lot of other things to buy.'

To which prudent speech George made no
answer, merely urged her through the door.

It could have been made for her, the fit was so
perfect, and there was a narrow-brimmed hat
which matched it exactly. In her excitement she
forgot to ask how much it cost, and it wasn't until
George was writing a cheque that she remembered
to ask. The sales lady told her in a sugary voice,
and Phoebe felt her cheeks pale. There would be
almost nothing left of her money and she still had
things to buy, things she simply had to have.
George had handed over the cheque by now, and
in any case, it would be difficult to do anything
about it now. She waited until they were outside
on the pavement: 'George—George, you don't
understand, when I've paid you back for that
outfit I won't have enough money to get some
things I just must have!'

He sounded very matter-of-fact. 'Suppose you

buy all you need now and when we get back home
we can settle the matter. You'll be getting an
allowance once we're married; you can pay me
back from that.'

'Oh, well, if you don't·mind . . .' She felt relief
surge through her.

'So what comes next? Shoes, gloves, purse?
Something pretty for visiting? Friends will call,
you know, and we'll get asked out. Let's look
around.'

Phoebe ended up with a Jaeger suit, several
sweaters, two pretty dresses which George assured
her were absolutely essential to her wardrobe, a
jersey dress in sapphire blue, and shoes—smart
brogues for the suit, brown court shoes and a
purse to go with them for the wedding, high-heeled
sandals for the dresses and because she had paused
to admire them as they left the shop, a ridiculous
pair of bedroom slippers, pink satin and hihg-
heeled.

After this orgy of spending Phoebe did her best
to call a halt. 'If I could just slip into Marks and
Spencer,' she suggested.

'Undies?' asked George placidly. 'Tights and so
on? This shop will do.' He gave her a gentle push
towards the door. 'Get all you want and I'll come
in and pay when you're ready. At least three of
everything,' he told her gravely with twinkling
eyes, 'and no cheeseparing!'

Well, thought Phoebe, inside the shop, staring at
the delicate wisps of garments on display, this was
no place where one could pare cheese. She would
be the rest of her life paying George back, but in
for a penny, in for a pound. Obediently she bought
three of everything, revelling in the reckless
extravagance. It was only when the bill was made
out and she saw the total that she had qualms. But

it was too late now; she went to the door and
George came in, made out a cheque without a
muscle of his face changing and then collected her
numerous parcels.

'You told me to buy three of everything, and I
did,' said Phoebe. 'It's the most wickedly expensive
shop I've ever been in—I almost came out without
buying anything.'

'I'm glad you didn't. Let's have tea somewhere
and make sure you've got everything you need.'

He took her to the University Arms and gave
her teacakes, hot and dripping with butter, and
then ticked off the items she had bought.

'Raincoat?' he wanted to know. 'Wellington
boots—for when you come with me on my rounds
and we have to walk through muddy
farmyards . . .'

Phoebe went delicately pink. 'Oh, may I come
with you sometimes? I'll like that.'

'Of course you'll come with me if you want to.
Dressing gown?'

She bit into a teacake. 'My mac isn't really
old—I haven't any wellies, though. I've got a
dressing gown . . .' She paused. It was a useful
garment, designed for warmth and hard wear and
a quite unsuitable covering for the nighties she had
bought.

'Right, we'll get those next.' He cast an eye at
the pile of elegant carrier bags. 'There's time
before the shops close.'

So she found herself the possessor of the latest
Burberry raincoat and a matching hat and scarf,
wellies and, lastly, a pink silk quilted dressing
gown which George, when asked, told her to buy.
On the way back to Woolpit Phoebe tried to add
up how much she had spent; it was an
astronomical sum.

Indoors, sitting in the sitting room with George, she broached the subject once again, and was told with kind firmness to wait until they were married and she had her allowance paid into the bank.

'Yes, but it's hundreds of pounds!'

'And I never spent them with greater pleasure.' He got up and went to the small rent table under the window and opened one of its drawers. 'If you don't like this tell me and we'll find something more to your taste. This was my grandmother's, and I'd like you to have it.'

It was a very beautiful ring; old-fashioned rose diamonds and rubies set in gold. Phoebe gave a gasp of delight and held out her hand. It fitted exactly. 'It's gorgeous,' she told him, 'and I like it very much. I'll take such care of it.'

He smiled at her. 'It suits your hand. You have pretty hands, Phoebe, has anyone ever told you that?'

She thought for a moment. 'No. I'm glad you think they're pretty, perhaps that'll make up for my ordinary face.'

'I can see that it's time someone told you that's a load of nonsense.' He leaned down and pulled her out of her chair. 'Let's have supper, then I'm going to walk you down to Nurse Wilkins'—I've got some work to do later on.'

Phoebe accepted that tranquilly. She had no illusions about their life together; she would learn to fit in to his way of living and learn not to mind if his work came between them. If she had loved him, she supposed, she would mind very much. As it was, she was quite prepared to take a back seat, be an understanding friend, there when wanted, but able to efface herself if it seemed the right thing to do. She hadn't seen the intent look he had bent on her when she had spoken, watching to see if she were disappointed.

Over their supper they fixed the date for the
wedding—the following week; Thursday morning
at ten o'clock. 'And we'll come straight back
here, Phoebe, I've got an appointment at
Stowmarket Hospital in the afternoon which I
can't miss, but I've fixed up a week's holiday—
we'll go over to Holland on the Saturday and
you'll be able to meet my mother and the family.'

She agreed readily, hiding twinges of uncer-
tainty. Suppose his mother didn't like her?
Suppose his family cold-shouldered her? She
hadn't the faintest idea what they would be like.
Of course, if they were all like him, that would be
all right. She cheered up at the thought and
presently declared that she was more than ready to
go to Nurse Wilkins'. There was still a lot of the
evening left and she would have liked to have
spent it all talking to George, but instead she
would unpack her parcels and try everything on
for Nurse Wilkins to see. She made no attempt to
linger, but wished him a quite brisk goodnight
with the observation that she wouldn't delay him
further, and went into the cottage and shut the
door. The doctor walked back to his own house,
his shoulders shaking with laughter. He had
enjoyed his afternoon, he felt sure he was going to
enjoy the rest of his life. Patience would be
required, of course, but he had plenty of that.

CHAPTER FOUR

PHOEBE had arranged to meet George at the church door. Mrs Thirsk would already be there, waiting for them, and Andrew Powers from Stowmarket, the doctor with whom George exchanged duties from time to time, would be there too. And at the last minute Nurse Wilkins, who had arranged her rounds to fit in. Phoebe walked to the church with her, feeling self-conscious in her new outfit, although as it happened there was no need, because there was no one about. At the church door George was waiting, sitting on a tombstone. He had taken surgery as usual but she was glad to see that he had dressed for the occasion. Indeed, she could find no fault with his grey suit; it was exquisitely cut and faultlessly tailored. She said hullo shyly and scarcely saw Nurse Wilkins slip past into the church.

George unfolded his length and took her hand. 'You look just as a bride should,' he observed. 'Let's go in, shall we?'

In the porch he reached for a small posy of flowers, lilies of the valley, early roses, hyacinths and freesias, put them into her hands and pushed the inner door open.

The church was full; the entire village must be there, thought Phoebe confusedly. If it hadn't been for George's hand on her arm, she might have turned and run away, but as it was, she walked down the short aisle beside him to where John Matthews was waiting for them.

She hardly heard a word of the short service.

She heard her voice, a little high, giving the right answers, and George's deliberate tones; she watched him put the ring on her finger in a kind of dream, signed the register and then walked out of the church, her arm tucked into his, looking half smilingly at the rows of faces in the pews.

At the church door she asked in a whisper: 'Did you know, George?'

'I suspected something.' He gave her arm a small squeeze. 'When you think about it, it was a pretty nice thing for them to do.'

'Yes. Where do we go now?'

'Oh, a drink with John and Andrew, and then we'll take ourselves off for lunch. It's our wedding day, you know, even though I've got surgery this evening. Mrs Thirsk and Nurse Wilkins will see that your things get brought over this afternoon, because of course you'll come back with me now.'

They had strolled down the church path and now most of the congregation had caught up with them and they were engulfed in congratulations and goodnatured greetings—even more good-natured when George caught sight of the pub's landlord and asked him to see that the drinks were on him for the rest of the day.

Presently they were free to walk on once more, to find that Mrs Thirsk, Nurse Wilkins and the two men were waiting for them. They drank champagne, discussing the wedding, until presently George. said: 'Phoebe and I are off now—take any calls, Andrew, won't you? I'll be back for surgery.'

They went to Wetheringsett Manor, not too far away, a nice country house standing in twenty acres, so that after lunch they were able to stroll around undisturbed. It was a splendid day for a wedding, as George pointed out; a blue sky and a sunshine bearing the early warmth of promised summer. They found a seat in a sunny corner and sat quietly, admiring the view, not talking much, but quite content with each other's company. Once or twice Phoebe looked at the ring on her finger and reminded herself that she was now Mrs Pritchard, although she didn't feel any different. They wandered back presently and had tea at the hotel, then got into the car and drove back to Woolpit.

While George was in the surgery, she unpacked her things in the pretty bedroom waiting for her. There was a bathroom beside it and George's bedroom on the other side, and presently she went exploring, to open two more doors on to two rooms at the back of the house, one very large, furnished with a pale wood she didn't recognise. The bed was covered with a quilted spread which matched the curtains and the carpet was soft and deep. Perhaps she and George would share it one day, but first, as he had said, they must get to know each other. Easy for him, she thought, hanging her new clothes in the roomy built-in cupboard lining one wall; he only had to get to know her, there wasn't anyone else, whereas she would have to meet his mother and his family, and in another country too. The thought was daunting and at the same time a challenge too. She paused in her unpacking and went to study herself in the long pier glass; clothes certainly did something for one, and as soon as she could, she would go to a good hairdresser and get her hair done.

She went down to the sitting room presently, feeling rather shy, to discover that George was still in the surgery. But Mrs Thirsk came from the kitchen, smiling broadly, to follow her into the sitting room and ask if she wanted anything.

'Doctor won't be long, Mrs Pritchard, he said I was to see that you had all you wanted.'

Phoebe said quickly: 'I'll wait for the doctor, Mrs Thirsk,' and then: 'Did you enjoy the wedding?'

'That I did, and so did everyone else.' She chuckled: 'Your face—so surprised you were! You looked very pretty too—you make a fine pair, you and the doctor, Mrs Pritchard.' She went to the door. 'I'd better be back in my kitchen—it's dinner you're having tonight, on account of the wedding—champagne too.'

George came presently. 'You look as though you've been here all my life,' he told her. Phoebe wasn't sure if that was a compliment, it made her feel like his favourite chair or a comfortable pair of old slippers, but she smiled and murmured something and accepted a glass of champagne that he offered her.

She murmured something too when he toasted their future, suddenly afraid that she had bitten off more than she could chew.

But George seemed to have no such qualms. He talked about the wedding, invited her to go round the house at her leisure and decide if she wanted any alterations in the furniture or decorating, and lastly mentioned casually that they would be going over to Holland in two days' time.

'Andrew Powers will take over my patients for a couple of weeks. We'll take the car and drive around so that you can see something of the country.'

'Shall we stay with your mother?' she asked.

'For some of the time, yes. I phoned her this morning early, and she's delighted at our news and looking forward to meeting you.' He refilled her glass. 'Can you drive a car, Phoebe?' She shook her head. 'No matter—you shall have lessons as soon as we get back. I'll run you into Stowmarket after I've done my morning round—I can spare an hour. You only need to go to the bank.'

'Yes—I'll be very quick. Should I close my account and open another one at your bank?'

'Yes, do that, will you? We'll discuss your finances at our leisure.'

Mrs Thirsk appeared then to tell them that dinner was waiting, and a splendid meal it turned out to be. The table held a centrepiece of flowers, and the silver and crystal glasses Phoebe had admired the very first time she had stayed to supper shone and gleamed. They began with hors d'oeuvres, went on to chicken à la king with asparagus and baby peas, and finished with a magnificent trifle. And when Mrs Thirsk came in to the room with the coffee, George told her to fetch a glass and the three of them finished the champagne. It was a pity that the doctor should have been called out to visit an urgent case before they left the table. Phoebe helped Mrs Thirsk clear and then went to sit with a book picked at random from the well stocked bookshelves in the small library behind the sitting-room, but she didn't read for more than a minute or two; she had a lot to think about. She was a practical girl; she decided that when they went to Stowmarket in the morning she would get herself some wool and knitting needles—she was quite good at following advanced patterns, she would get something really complicated which would keep her occupied. She would have a chat with Mrs Thirsk too, because she couldn't sit idle all day; there must be several small chores she could take over without upsetting the housekeeping. How fortunate that they liked each other.

She sat on, oblivious of the time, until Mrs Thirsk came in to ask her if she would like more coffee.

Phoebe looked at the clock and saw that it was already half-past ten. George had been gone a long time. 'I'll wait up for a bit,' she said. 'Do you usually go to bed if the doctor's not here?'

Mrs Thirsk nodded. 'He could be out till all hours. I'll lock up everything but the front door and take myself to bed. You'll be all right, Mrs Pritchard?'

'I'm not sleepy yet—I'll wait a bit longer and then go up. What about the morning, Mrs Thirsk?'

'I'll call you at seven o'clock, ma'am—breakfast at half past so that the doctor has time to read his post and that before surgery. Is that too early?'

'No—I had to get up at half-past six in the hospital, I shan't mind at all.' They wished each other goodnight and Mrs Thirsk went back to her kitchen, and presently Phoebe heard her deliberate tread on the back stairs.

She read for a while after that and was surprised to find that an hour had gone by. She was sleepy now and closed the book and her eyes with it, so that she didn't hear George come quietly into his house. She did wake up, however, as he came into the room. The look on his face startled her. He was standing in the doorway, frowning, looking so stern that she sat up straight in her chair.

'My dear girl, it's after midnight—you should be in bed!'

She found herself apologising. 'I'm sorry—I went to sleep over my book.' She added, in the hope that it might put things right: 'I didn't mean to wait up for you.'

His cool voice chilled her. 'No? I hardly expected you to be a wife who expects to check every breath her husband takes.'

His words hurt her so much that she could have wept, but that wouldn't help matters; she said pleasantly: 'I can promise you I won't do that.' She got to her feet and put the book carefully on the lamp table. 'My goodness, I'm asleep on my feet—it's been a long day hasn't it? Goodnight, George.'

She gave him a bright smile and went upstairs and into her room. Once there, she undressed in a fury of haste, jumped into bed and for no reason which she could think of, had a good cry.

She was at the breakfast table next morning only minutes after George, wished him a good morning, exchanged the same with Mrs Thirsk, and applied herself to coffee and toast.

George glanced up from his letters. 'That's an inadequate breakfast,' he pointed out. 'I hope you'll do better tomorrow.' He studied her rather pale face. 'You slept well?'

'Like a log,' she assured him cheerfully, and buttered more toast.

George put down his letter. 'I do apologise for last night, Phoebe, it was unpardonable of me.'

'That's all right; I expect you'd forgotten that I was here. I daresay I shall take a bit of getting used to.'

He said seriously: 'Yes, I think I must agree with you there. All the same, I'm sorry. It wasn't much of an end to our wedding day.'

She thought of several replies to that, none of them suitable. 'What time do you want me to be ready this morning?' she asked.

'Oh, around twelve, I should imagine.' He glanced at the clock. 'I must go; I've got one or two matters to attend to before I start work.' He got up and as he passed her, paused and put a hand on her shoulder. 'Friends?' he asked.

She smiled up at him. 'Well, of course, George.'

After he had gone she poured herself another cup of coffee. There would be pitfalls ahead; to be expected, of course, but she would have to be prepared for those. Even though they liked each other, felt as though they had known each other for a long time, they still didn't know much about each other. She finished her coffee and carried the tray out to the kitchen where Mrs Thirsk was cutting up rhubarb at the table and Susan, of all people, was getting ready to wash up at the sink.

'Why, Susan!' cried Phoebe. 'Good morning— how nice to see you.'

Susan grinned, but it was the housekeeper who answered. 'There weren't no chance to tell you yesterday, ma'am, but the doctor suggested that I might like to have Susan mornings now she's not wanted across the green. And that reminds me, I'm to go with you and help you pack up. When shall that be, ma'am?'

'When you've got time, Mrs Thirsk. And is there anything I can do?'

'Well, this morning, there's not much else than the flowers. Doctor, he likes flowers round the house and there's plenty in the garden, but if it suits you we could go now to Miss James's house . . .'

'That suits me fine. It'll only take me twenty minutes or so.' The pair of them started for the door. 'And while I'm doing it, will you tell me your routine for the day and tell me how I can best help?'

'That I will gladly.' Mrs Thirsk rolled down her sleeves and got a cardigan from behind the door. 'The key's on the hall table,' she observed.

Aunt Kate's house felt chill and unlived-in as Phoebe unlocked the door. She was glad to hurry

upstairs and get her case and start to pack the rest
of her clothes while Mrs Thirsk peered into
drawers and cupboards to make sure that nothing
was left behind. 'Let's hope a respectable nice
couple will buy the place,' she observed as Phoebe
shut the lid. She picked up the case and followed
Phoebe downstairs.

'Now if you like to put these things away,
ma'am, I'll get the coffee ready—the doctor likes a
cup when he finishes surgery and there weren't
many patients this morning—the evening is always
busy when the men have finished work. Will you
want lunch at one o'clock, same as usual?'

'I expect so, Mrs Thirsk. We're going to
Stowmarket as soon as the doctor's done his visits,
but we'll only be there for a very short time. I
expect we'd better ask, hadn't we?'

By the time Phoebe had put away her things,
surgery was over, She could hear George's voice
downstairs and when she went down it was to find
him in the sitting room, sitting on the edge of the
Pembroke table under the window with Beauty at
his feet. He was his old placid self, she saw with
relief, and smiled. 'Shall I get the coffee, or does
Mrs Thirsk bring it?' she asked.

'She'll bring it. You've fetched your things?'

'Yes, I've been putting them away.'

He nodded. 'Can you be ready by twelve sharp?
Half an hour will be time enough in Stowmarket,
won't it?'

'Oh yes.' It looked as though she wouldn't have
time to buy wool and needles unless the bank
business was dealt with quickly.

As it turned out, it took barely ten minutes.
Phoebe skipped down the street, found wool,
needles and a pattern complicated enough to keep
her busy for days on end, and hurried back to

where the car was parked. George was at the
wheel, his face calm and patient. 'Five minutes to
spare,' he said as he opened the door for her.
'Everything all right?'

'Yes, thanks. It'll take about a week, they said.'

He was already driving out of the town, back to
Woolpit. 'Well, there's no hurry, I've opened an
account for you at my—our bank, and your
allowance will be paid in each month. Mrs Thirsk
has always kept the household accounts and given
me the bills at the end of every month; she's hated
that side of housekeeping—do you think you could
cope?'

'I'd like to. She'll show me what to do?'

'Yes, of course, and when I've got an hour or
two, I'll give you some idea of how much you can
spend on housekeeping. We'll go on paying the
bills each month, but you can do it instead of me.'

He glanced sideways at Phoebe's expressive face
and smiled a little. 'You look pleased,' he
observed.

'Well, I am—I mean, there must be several
things I can do to help you and Mrs Thirsk.' She
paused. 'It was nice to see Susan in the kitchen.
She would have been out of work . . .'

He made no answer. Presently he asked if she
had all she wanted for their trip to Holland. 'We'll
go via Harwich tomorrow evening,' he told her.
'We'll be gone for about ten days; if you need any
more clothes we can get them while we're there.'

'I've got enough, I'm sure, only I haven't got a
dress for the evening, but I don't suppose I'll need
one.'

He glanced at her, very smart in her new outfit
and shining shoes. 'Well, we might go dancing one
evening. John Matthews is taking his wife to Bury
St Edmunds tomorrow morning—she has to go to

the dentist—he'll give you a lift and you'll be back
before lunch.'

Phoebe thought of the few pounds in her purse;
her account wouldn't be cleared yet and hadn't she
handed her cheque book in that very morning and
she wouldn't get the new one in time. She was
wondering what to say when he went on: 'I'll let
you have some cash.'

'Yes, well—thank you, George, but I owe you
an awful lot of money already.'

'Ah yes—we'll have time to sort that out when
we're on holiday, won't we? Would a hundred
pounds be enough?'

'A hundred?' squeaked Phoebe. 'My goodness,
that's far too much!'

'Then get two dresses.' He swept the car to a
halt before the house and they got out.

She asked carefully as they went indoors. 'Do
you want me to pack for you, George?'

He stopped, his hand on the surgery door. 'Er—
don't bother, my dear. I'll throw a few things into
a bag tomorrow. Lunch in five minutes? I must
phone . . .'

Phoebe packed after lunch, all her lovely new
things, glad at least that her case wasn't too
shabby. But she would have to get an overnight
bag in the morning if they were going on the night
boat. She sat down and did sums on the back of
an envelope and found that she was hopelessly in
debt to George; probably it would take her
months and months to pay him back.

He gave her the money casually while they were
waiting for their supper that evening, and all she
could do was to thank him; something in his face
stopped her from saying anything else. Later on,
when she felt quite at ease with him, she would ask
him how he would like her to repay him.

She didn't suppose he was too badly off, but he had the house to maintain and Mrs Thirsk to pay and the car to run, and she couldn't help but see that he wore beautifully tailored clothes which must cost a good deal. But even if he lived comfortably, she was an extra expense now, and she had no intention of being a burden on him. She made a careful note of her debt and stowed it away in her handbag so that when a suitable moment cropped up, she would be ready.

The Reverend John Matthews collected her the next morning at nine o'clock. He had his wife with him, miserable with toothache but all agog, just the same, over the wedding. It was the sole topic of conversation until they reached Bury St Edmunds, where they set her down near the shops and promised to wait for her in the car park. 'But not later than half past twelve,' she was warned.

'I'll be there at twelve at the latest,' she promised.

She didn't know the town, but the shops looked satisfactory. She bought her overnight bag and then studied the windows of several boutiques, and with an eye on the clock chose one. She was fortunate in her choice; the turquoise blue crêpe dress she tried on fitted her to perfection. It was suitable, she felt, for a first meeting with George's mother, as it was simply cut and had style. There was enough money over for her to buy a dark green taffeta skirt and a chiffon blouse to go with it. She was aware that her purchases were perhaps a little old for her, but she was, after all, a married woman. She resolutely refused to try on the more youthful clothes the sales lady showed her and found her way back to the car park, arriving, most luckily, at the same time as the Matthews.

George wasn't back from his visits when she

went into the house. She packed the dress and skirt and blouse, added some last-minute odds and ends and sat down to wait for him.

'Find what you wanted?' he asked when he got home.

'Yes, thank you.' The doubt at the back of her mind showed through and he gave her a quick glance, although he said nothing, but over lunch he observed that he hadn't given her a wedding present yet. 'We'll go shopping, and you can spread yourself.'

'But I've already done that,' she protested. 'I've never had so many new clothes!'

'No? Well, I've a great many friends and acquaintances, Phoebe, we shall go out quite a bit, you know, so you'll need clothes.'

She agreed meekly and wondered what he had thought of her dull dresses. Too late, she wished she had agreed to the sales lady's advice in the boutique and bought one of the more spectacular dresses she had been shown. On the other hand, she wanted most desperately that his mother should like her, and she might be a lady who had conservative ideas about dress.

It wasn't a great distance to Harwich. They left after George had done his evening clinic and conferred with Andrew Powers. To Phoebe, on tenterhooks to be gone, George seemed almost too casual, and yet they arrived at the quay in plenty of time. She hadn't been out of England before. The Customs and passport procedures were strange and exciting; she watched her visitor's passport, which they had got in Cambridge, being stamped and quite expected that her case would be opened and inspected. But no one did anything, so they went on board, parked the car in the car deck and climbed the stairs to the decks above. She

hadn't known what to expect; certainly she had
had no idea that George would have got
everything so well organised. They were taken at
once to their cabins, where she had laid out what
she needed for the night, and then, in response to
George's knock, accompanied him to the restaurant, where they had had a late supper and then
gone on deck to watch the last of the lights from
the fast receding shore.

She slept like a top, had eaten an early breakfast
with George and then had gone to hang over the
side to watch the ferry docking. And George had
been very patient and kind, explaining everything
to her and then taking her down to the car.

There was no hold-up going through Customs,
and they were away, driving away from the Hook,
in no time at all. It was only then that Phoebe
said: 'I don't really know where we're going.'

'Hilversum—an hour more or less on the
motorway. We'll be there for coffee.'

'Your mother lives in Hilversum?'

'Yes, she has a house there, left to her by my
grandfather—my Dutch grandfather. She spends
part of each year there. It's a pleasant town and
the country round it is charming, wooded and
peaceful, not at all like this.' He nodded at the flat
water meadows they were passing, with the black
and white cows scattered thickly and the farms
with their great barns lying back from the road.
'This is the Holland people always expect to see,
but although it's so small, the north and the part
we call the Veluwe are quite different. I'll drive
you there, at this time of the year it's delightful.'

Phoebe turned to look at his placid profile.
'George, do you feel more Dutch than English?'

He laughed. 'I suppose when I'm in Holland I
feel Dutch, but in England I'm as English as the

next man. But don't worry, Mother speaks excellent English and you'll have no difficulty in the shops—Dutch isn't an easy language to learn, so most people take care to learn some English at least.'

They were going through Rotterdam by now. Phoebe wondered how he could find his way so easily through the busy streets, but presently they were free of the city, racing along towards Utrecht.

'It's a pity the motorways bypass the towns and villages,' observed George, 'but I promise you we'll take the side roads when we go on a sightseeing tour. There's Gouda to the right and there are some rather pretty lakes a little further on.'

. They were going so fast that she barely glimpsed them, and in no time at all they were at the roundabout outside Utrecht, not going into the city but taking the road round it and then striking north. The country was green and wooded now, and presently as they reached the outskirts of Hilversum, the trees crept down to the verge of the motorway, opening into a wide, tree-lined road taking them into the town.

The road was lined with solid mansions standing in well kept grounds, each with a wide gateway leading up to the house. The road seemed to go on for ever, and Phoebe asked: 'Is this Hilversum? There's no town . . .'

'It's a short distance ahead.' George swept the car between stone pillars and into a gravel drive leading to a magnificent house standing well back from the road. Phoebe caught her breath. 'Is this it? Is this where your mother lives?'

'Yes, it's home to me too when I'm in Holland.' He undid her seat-belt and leaned across to open her door and got out himself. She was glad of his

friendly hand on her arm as they went up the wide
steps to the massive door. She said nervously,
laughing a little: 'It's the kind of door you expect a
butler to open,' and then gave a gasp as it was
thrown wide by a tall, reedy man, no longer
young, dressed in a black jacket and striped
trousers.

'Phoebe, this is Ulco, who has been with the
family since I was a very small boy. He is also one
of my greatest friends.' George's voice was very
kind. 'Ulco, this is my wife.'

Phoebe held out a hand and smiled from a
flushed face. 'How do you do, Ulco—I'm sorry,
but I can't speak any Dutch.'

'I speak a little English,' Ulco told her gravely,
'and I am most happy to welcome you, Mrs
Pritchard.' He smiled at her then and her own
uncertain smile widened. 'Mrs Pritchard senior is
in the drawing-room, Mr George.'

He led the way across the wide high-ceilinged
hall, with its polished wooden floor scattered
with rugs and its panelled walls hung with
portraits. Phoebe, still firmly held by George's
hand, had no time to take it all in. She felt like
someone leaving the dentist's waiting room for
the dental chair, only worse. But not for long.
The double doors they were approaching were
suddenly flung wide and a comfortably plump
lady darted out. She was no taller than Phoebe
and although elegantly dressed, exuded an air of
cosiness which Phoebe found distinctly heart-
ening. She cried: 'George, dear George!' and
stood on tiptoe to embrace him before turning to
fling her arms round Phoebe. 'And Phoebe—so
exactly as George has described you! Welcome,
my dear, I'm so very happy to meet you.' She
said something to Ulco and led the way into the

drawing-room, a vast apartment, furnished with
a nicely balanced mixture of comfortable sofas
and easy chairs and quite beautiful antiques.
George had taken his hand from her arm with a
little chuckle, and it was his mother who led
Phoebe to a handsome velvet-covered sofa and
sat her down, then sat beside her, leaving her
son to settle himself in the great winged chair
opposite.

The next few minutes were taken up with
questions about their journey and how was
Woolpit and Mrs Thirsk and what had they done
with Beauty while they were away; and was
George's practice flourishing, and could Phoebe
bear it if her mother-in-law invited herself for a
week or two later on? 'I've a house in
Grantchester,' explained that lady. 'I live there
quite a lot, you know, but I'd love to stay with you
both.' She broke off as Ulco came in with the
coffee tray and then rattled on happily about
various members of the family, her friends, people
George knew . . . 'I'm giving a party for you both,'
she told them, 'next week—we'll have a few friends
and the family to dinner and everyone else can
come later on.' She turned to Phoebe and smiled,
her eyes as startlingly blue as her son's. 'I want
you to meet them all,' she told her, 'I'm so proud
of having a daughter-in-law.'

Presently she took Phoebe upstairs, mounting
the grand sweep of the staircase with the lightness
of a girl. The gallery above the hall was wide with
a number of doors leading from it as well as
several corridors. Mrs Pritchard opened a door
and ushered Phoebe inside. 'Here you are,' she
said happily. 'There's a bathroom through that
door and George is next to that. Ring for anything
you want—everyone in the house speaks a little

English, and George will help, of course. I expect
you'd like to tidy up after that long journey, but
come down as soon as you like, my dear.'

Left alone, Phoebe looked around her. The room
was large, furnished with great taste and luxury, and
the bathroom was equally splendid. She went to
look out of the window at the formal garden below,
bright with spring flowers, the lawns like velvet.
After a few minutes she washed her hands and face
and sat down to do her hair and put on fresh
make-up. That done, she made no effort to move,
but sat there, staring at her reflection in the big
winged mirror. When someone tapped on the door,
she said, 'Come in,' without bothering to look
round, and only when George sat down on the side
of the bed did she look at him.

'Why didn't you tell me?' she asked.

He didn't pretend not to understand her. 'Oh,
several reasons—you see, Phoebe, this is my home
as well as England. I spent a good deal of my
boyhood here—school holidays and so on. My
father was happy here too, you know. I suppose to
you it seems a little grand, but to me it's just my
second home. I hope you'll come to love it too.'

She asked quietly: 'George, is your mother rich?'

'Yes. Father had money and she comes from an
old Dutch family—Thyss van Linke. She's a
baroness in her own right and has, even for these
days, a sizeable fortune.'

Phoebe opened her mouth to speak, but he
didn't give her the chance. 'I have a good deal of
money too, my dear, but I've never let it influence
my life. I hope it won't make any difference to
you, Phoebe.'

'Well, no, it won't once I've got used to it. Only
I wish you'd told me before—before we got
married.'

'Then you might not have married me.' He
smiled at her and got up from the bed. 'Come
downstairs, Mother's dying to talk to you. Are
you tired ? You can have a nap if you'd like to.'

She looked astonished. 'Tired? Not a bit.' She
laughed a little. 'Only grannies take naps ...' She
pinkened.

'And you're not a granny yet,' finished George
smoothly.

The day passed pleasantly. After lunch, Phoebe
was taken on a tour of the house and then with
George strolled round the large garden. The
boundary bordered on woods, pine trees mostly;
there was a little wicket gate which opened out on
to a bridle path, and George told her they could
walk for miles if they felt so inclined. 'But not
today—a quiet evening and early bed for you,
Phoebe, it's been a long day.'

'But a lovely one,' said Phoebe, and then,
worriedly: 'I do hope I've got the right clothes.'

He took her arm. 'I think we might go
shopping tomorrow. Ask mother what you
should wear—is it the party you're worried
about?'

She thought how kind he was to bother himself
about it. 'Yes. I bought a dress—I thought it
would be suitable for a doctor's wife.' She didn't
see his smile. 'But when I went to the party with—
with Basil, the girls were wearing very smart
dresses or trouser suits, perhaps they're very smart
here, too?'

'Well, I daresay the younger women will be,'
observed George placidly, then added: 'I dislike
trouser suits.'

'Well, I won't buy one, then,' conceded Phoebe,
'I might not have to buy anything, your mother
might think the one I've got is quite suitable—it

would be an awful waste if I don't wear it. I've got a skirt and a blouse too.'

His lips twitched. 'Well, shall we see what Mother says?' he suggested.

Phoebe changed into one of the pretty dresses she had bought in Cambridge for dinner that evening, and was relieved to find that Mrs Pritchard was wearing something similar. They finished dinner and were in the drawing room drinking their coffee when visitors arrived—an elderly man and woman and a pretty girl, older than Phoebe but beautifully turned out. Old friends, explained George, shaking hands and then kissing the girl: Mijnheer and Mevrouw van Renkel and their daughter Corina. They were offered coffee and sat drinking it, speaking English but occasionally switching over to Dutch, only to stop and apologise to Phoebe because she couldn't understand a word. Corina, she noticed, did that more often than anyone else, smiling at her with a kind of sly amusement. She was glad when the van Renkels got up to go and then put quite out of countenance when Corina declared that she was going to stay for a little longer, explaining that her parents could call for her on their way back from a visit to friends. Neither Mrs Pritchard or George showed anything but pleasure at her decision, and they sat around talking, carefully including Phoebe, until Mrs Pritchard suggested that if Phoebe was going shopping in the morning, they had better go upstairs and look at her dresses. Phoebe followed her out of the room, reluctant to leave George with Corina, aware that she was being foolish and quite startled at her strong feeling of annoyance. But she didn't let Mrs Pritchard notice that, but followed her obediently to her room, where she took out the blue dress and, when encouraged to do so, put it on.

'A very pretty dress, my dear,' pronounced Mrs

Pritchard, 'but it doesn't do you justice. You're too thin, of course, but you've got a lovely figure and some of the clothes these days are charming for the young. Get something with big sleeves and a lower neckline, and you're slim enough to wear one of those lovely full skirts. What else have you got?'

Phoebe produced the skirt and then the blouse. 'You have good taste, my dear, but you're far too young to wear anything like that. You shall go with George tomorrow—and mind you take his advice!'

They went downstairs presently and found Corina still there, a fact which Mrs Pritchard remarked upon in her friendly way. 'Shall I get Ulco to drive you back?' she suggested. 'George and Phoebe have had a long day . . .'

Perhaps it was fortunate that Corina's parents returned at that moment, because Phoebe was sure that George was on the point of offering to drive the girl home himself. As it was, Corina was swept away after ten minutes or so and Ulco, without being asked, came in with more coffee. The three of them sat talking for another half hour or so until George said abruptly: 'You're already almost asleep on your feet, my dear. Go to bed.'

'Of course you must,' agreed Mrs Pritchard, 'especially as you're going shopping tomorrow. George, Phoebe needs quite a few things—take her into Hilversum. There's Gig's boutique and Haan's and de Cuyp, one of them should be able to fit her out.' She took Phoebe's hand and said kindly: 'That's a Jaeger suit hanging in your closet, isn't it? My favourite—and always in such excellent taste.' She leaned forward and kissed Phoebe. 'My dear, don't think I'm patronising you—you're so sweet, and just the daughter I would have so loved to have had.'

Phoebe kissed the beautifully made up cheek. 'If you don't mind,' she said shyly, 'I'd like to think of you as Mother. I can hardly remember my own, you know.'

She said goodnight and George opened the door for her and dropped a kiss on her cheek as she paused there. 'Sleep well,' he said in his kind voice.

There was no reason why she shouldn't have done just that. Instead, she lay awake for a long time in her luxurious bed, beset by doubts. The biggest doubt, for some reason she couldn't fathom, was Corina.

CHAPTER FIVE

TWENTY-four hours later, Phoebe was back in bed again, but with far different thoughts. It had been an exciting day and a very happy one, and she hadn't given Corina van Renkel a single thought. Now she lay, determined not to go to sleep until she had gone over every minute of it. They had left the house shortly after a leisurely breakfast and driven the short distance to the centre of the town. She had been surprised to find it so modern, but she had liked it at once. With the car parked in Het Hof Holland hotel car park, they had had coffee, booked a table for lunch and gone in search of the boutiques. She hadn't expected George to take such an interest in what she bought; indeed, he picked out several dresses which she had looked at longingly but considered too much in the forefront of fashion for herself. He had insisted, with a placid determination she couldn't ignore, that she tried them on, and when she paraded in them, observed that they suited her very well. They were certainly like nothing she had ever worn before—the materials silky and gorgeous colours, cut so cunningly that she had to admit that they did something for her. She felt a different girl, looking at the transformation in the enormous mirror.

They took the dresses back to the car and Phoebe said diffidently, 'Shall I find a hairdresser and have something done to my hair?' She had been very surprised at George's quite emphatic refusal.

'Your hair is exactly right,' he told her, 'and it suits you. Have it washed and so on if you like, but don't dare have it curled and waved.' They had been strolling along, glancing in shop windows, and he had stopped to look at a silvery-grey dress, cast negligently over a gilt chair in a boutique window. 'Now that,' he had told her, 'is just made for you. Let's get it.'

So she had acquired yet another dress, a dream of a dress, she mused; soft silky pleats and a gorgeous belt. They had had lunch after that and he had suggested that they should drive round for a while. He had taken her to Loenen along the country roads and down the River Vecht, with its country houses bordering the river, and crossed to the other side and gone through Maarssen. They drove slowly so that she could see the lakes, and so to Tienhoven, past the airfield and on to Hilversum, where George had parked the car once more and had taken her to an elegant little tea-shop, where she had eaten an enormous cream cake and, when pressed, a second.

'I'm greedy,' she observed, 'only they are sheer heaven.' She plunged her fork into the mountain of delicate pastry. 'I shall get fat, and it will serve me right!'

George had laughed. 'You're very satisfactory as you are, but a few more pounds wouldn't come amiss, and it's delightful to be with a girl who doesn't pick at dry biscuits and lettuce leaves.'

She had paused, the fork halfway to her mouth. 'Oh—did you go out with girls—a girl, who did that?'

He had laughed again. 'Oh, several.' He added: 'That was a long time ago, Phoebe.'

A very satisfactory answer. She smiled sleepily and closed her eyes.

There were uncles and aunts and cousins coming to lunch the next day. It was a chilly, blustery morning and Phoebe wore the Jaeger suit, and was rewarded by George's smiling approval and his mother's, 'Charming—how well it suits you, my dear.' But before the guests arrived she put on a raincoat, tied a scarf over her head and went for a long walk with George through the wicket gate and into the dripping woods behind the house. It was very quiet there, the trodden earth paths soft and damp underfoot.

'We might as well have our little chat about ways and means,' George observed. He had put a hand on her shoulder and slowed his stride to fit her smaller steps. He talked calmly for some time and she listened carefully, for he was explaining how his family had become wealthy. It went back a long way. His father's forebears had been what Phoebe privately called landed gentry and had invested wisely in the first railways. There had always been doctors in the family, he explained, who had done well and added to the family fortunes, and his mother—well, her family had made its fortune in the Dutch East Indies in the seventeenth century and prudently added to it over the centuries. 'And of course there aren't so many children nowadays. Once upon a time the money had to be divided between a dozen or more, now the family is large enough, but half the size it was a hundred years ago. So there's more money for all of us, if you understand me.'

'Yes—well, I suppose I'll get used to that.'

Her companion's face expressed faint arrogance. 'Naturally you will. You said you would like to help with the practice. I should be glad of that—of course there's Nurse Wilkins, but just lately I've been wondering if I should take on a nurse for the surgery. It would save a good deal of time—injections, bandaging and so on, holding babies, soothing anxious mothers ... Would you like to do that? It would still leave you plenty of time to do what you wanted, and I doubt if I should need you at evening surgery.'

Phoebe felt a wave of pleasure. 'Oh, I would like that. I'm not trained, though I learnt to bandage, and I can give injections and that kind of thing.'

'That sounds just right. Shall we give it a try?'

She agreed happily, and they retraced their steps.

They reached the house a few minutes before the first of the family arrived. Oom Charles and Tante Beatrix came first; a baron and baroness, Phoebe guessed from Ulco's announcement, although they didn't look like the part. Oom Charles strongly resembled his nephew, although his hair was grey and he stooped a little, and his wife was small and mouselike. She had barely exchanged polite nothings with them when two young women and a youngish man came in.

'Cousins,' murmured George in her ear. Juliana, tall and imposingly built and dressed rather strangely in an enormous cloak, a wide-brimmed felt hat and a vivid green dress; Sibilla, a smaller, paler edition of her sister and dressed, like Phoebe, in a classic suit, and lastly Cornelius, bearing a strong family likeness to George although he was shorter and more solidly built. Juliana was an artist, which might account for her rather startling clothes, thought Phoebe. Her sister did nothing; she was engaged to be married and invited Phoebe and George to the wedding, an invitation which George accepted at once before Cornelius joined them.

Ulco was offering drinks when the last of the

guests arrived—another aunt, Mrs Pritchard's sister, and very like her in appearance, accompanied by her daughter and her husband, and a tall white-haired old lady, very upright and dignified. 'Grandmother,' said George in Phoebe's ear. 'She doesn't go out much, she's come to look you over, my dear.'

She couldn't be worse than Aunt Kate, thought Phoebe as she stood quietly while the old lady's blue eyes examined her slowly.

'You may kiss me, Phoebe,' said George's grandmother.

Phoebe planted a light kiss on a nicely made up cheek and smiled, because she couldn't think of anything to say to fit the occasion. It seemed to have been the right thing to do, for the old lady nodded her stately head, offered a cheek to her grandson and said something to him in Dutch. He answered in the same language as they both looked at her. 'It's all right,' he explained. 'We're agreeing that you'll make me a very good wife.'

He smiled as he spoke and took her hand and held it quite unselfconsciously, and Phoebe, for the first time since they had married, felt wholly happy, although she had no idea why.

Lunch was a lengthy meal with a great deal of talk, almost all of it in English. Phoebe, sitting beside George at his place at the head of the table, with an uncle on either side, enjoyed herself. True, it was rather like being in a dream, but it was a nice dream, and she supposed, with her usual calm, that she would get used to living in the lap of luxury in time—after all, everyone else there took it for granted. Besides, even if George was rich, his home in Woolpit, although the ultimate in comfort, was . . . Her thoughts were interrupted by

George saying quietly: 'This is delightful, isn't it, Phoebe, but I have a great fondness for my own home in Woolpit.'

She turned surprised grey eyes on his. 'How did you know what I was thinking?' she asked.

'Your face is very expressive. I think I shall always know.' He told her.

The afternoon was spent pleasantly. One by one the aunts and uncles and cousins came and sat by Phoebe and cross-examined her in the kindliest possible way, always finishing by saying that George must give himself another holiday soon and bring her over to Holland for a long visit. They all lived in different parts of the country; Groningen, in the north, near the Hague, and at Rhenen on the Rhine. Grandmother lived in Friesland, they explained, by herself, if you discounted the companion who had been with her for ever. And Phoebe had an invitation from the old lady too, before she took her departure with a good deal of ceremony, driving away in an elderly Daimler driven by an elderly chauffeur. 'You'll visit me,' Phoebe had been told. 'George shall bring you over as soon as he can arrange it.' She had held Phoebe's eyes with a piercing stare. 'I am devoted to George, as I am sure you are also, my dear.'

Phoebe had the extraordinary feeling that a large bubble had burst somewhere inside her. She went very red and found that she hadn't enough breath. Something had just been made very plain to her. She was devoted to George too—more than that, she was besotted, hopelessly in love with him, and how was it possible that she hadn't discovered it until that very minute?

She went on staring at the old lady, while colour rushed into her face and then ebbed away, leaving it very pale. George's grandmother said nothing for a moment. 'I can see that we agree, my dear.' She offered a cheek to be kissed as George came towards them. She took his arm and went out to where her car was waiting.

When everyone had gone, they went for another walk. It was much easier, Phoebe decided, to walk and talk without having to look at him most of the time. They discussed his family in a mild sort of way, a subject which took them comfortably back to the house for a late tea.

'A quiet evening at home,' observed George with satisfaction, his eyes on Phoebe's face.

Only as it turned out it wasn't that at all. They were still sitting idly long after the tea tray had been taken away, when they heard a car turn into the drive and stop at the house. George didn't move, and Phoebe, taking a quick look at him, could see no change in his expression; all the same, it seemed that he was annoyed.

He said quietly. 'Kasper—were you expecting him, mother?'

His mother frowned slightly, 'No, dear,' then turned her head as Ulco came in to inform them all quietly that Mijnheer Kasper Thyss van Linke had arrived. He opened the door a little wider to allow the young man behind him to enter the room.

There was only one description that fitted him; tall, dark and handsome, for he was all three. What was more, he was smiling with such charm that he would have wrung equal smiles from the most ill-natured.

Something George was not. He got to his feet, topping their visitor by several inches. 'An unexpected pleasure, Kasper.' His voice was placid and he was smiling too, as his cousin crossed the room to kiss Mevrouw Thyss van Linke's cheek. 'You must meet my wife—Phoebe, this is Kasper, another cousin.'

Phoebe shook hands, going a little pink under the frankly interested gaze of his dark eyes, and wondered if George was going to enlarge on his rather uninformative introduction. Apparently not. She withdrew her hand, held a little too long, and regained her usual calm, despite her pink cheeks.

'How do you do? George, what a large family you have!' She smiled across the room at him and caught his curiously intent look. I wish I didn't blush, she thought, like a silly schoolgirl.

She didn't want to meet that dark gaze again, but she had to, for Kasper was speaking.

'But not so many of us that we cannot welcome such a charming addition to the family.' He glanced at George. 'My congratulations, George. What a pity your wedding was so quiet—I would have enjoyed being your best man. Are you staying here for long?'

'A few days so that Phoebe can meet as many of us as possible. And isn't it about time we danced at your wedding, Kasper?'

It was then that Phoebe realised that George didn't like him. There was nothing in his manner to betray it; she supposed that when you loved someone you acquired an extra sense which made you aware of their feelings even if they were well hidden.

'Time enough, George, though now that I've met my new cousin, I'm full of regret that I didn't see her first—now I have lost my heart too late!'

He thumped his chest so dramatically that Phoebe giggled. He was joking, of course—but all the same a small sneaking wish that George would lose his heart too, and not as a joke, crept into her head. She suppressed it at once as being disloyal, and felt relief when George laughed and his mother smiled.

'You'll stay to dinner, Kasper?' she asked, and George followed that with: 'What about a drink?'

'I hoped you would ask me. I'm on my way to Rhenen.' He turned to Phoebe sitting quietly, her colour once more normal. 'I live there. You must come and see it one day—it's on the Rhine and the country is charming.'

And Phoebe, anxious to return to a casual conversation, said readily: 'Oh, yes, weren't there bishops there once upon a time?'

He looked surprised. 'You've been there? You know Holland?'

'No, but when I knew we would be coming here, I read one or two books.'

She accepted a glass of sherry from George and felt relief as he swept them all into an easy conversation with apparently no effort at all. And presently his mother went away to tidy herself for dinner and Phoebe went with her, wanting to stay with George but anxious to get away from Kasper, who unsettled her so. She was quite sure she didn't like him, but he certainly unsettled her.

'I shall change,' declared Mevrouw Thyss van Linke. 'Put on one of your pretty dresses, child.'

Phoebe took great pains with her face and her hair. Surveying her person in the lovely old pier-glass in her room, she felt almost content with her appearance. True, she had no looks to speak of, but she had made the most of what she had, and surely George would notice . . .

She went slowly downstairs and found no one in the drawing room but Kasper. He came to meet her as she crossed the room and took a hand and held it between his own.

'That's a lovely dress, and a lovely girl in it,' he told her.

Phoebe tugged to free her hand, but he didn't let go. 'It's kind of you to say so, but I'm not lovely.' Her voice was tart. 'Besides, I don't think I like that kind of compliment.' She gave another tug. 'And I'd like my hand back.'

He paid no heed to her, looking over her shoulder and smiling.

'George, my ego is crushed—I don't think Phoebe likes me.'

He let her hand go then and she said quietly, not looking at George: 'I have to know people before I like them.' She smiled as she said it because Kasper was undoubtedly charming and she didn't want to hurt his feelings.

He didn't appear to be in the least put out. 'You've known each other for a long time?' he asked casually.

George caught her eye and smiled faintly. 'Oh yes, although I must point out that time doesn't have much to do with it, does it, my dear?'

Phoebe wished with all her heart that she was his dear as she agreed fervently and crossed the room to slip a hand into his. Its large firmness closed reassuringly round it, but only for a moment, for his mother joined them and he went to pour her drink, leaving her to sit rather uneasily and talk nothings until Ulco announced that dinner was served.

It was during dinner that Corina's name cropped up. 'Seen anything of Corina?' asked Kasper casually. 'Always great pals, weren't you? When I saw her a month or so ago, she was babbling on about paying you a visit.'

'Corina was here yesterday. A pity you missed her—the girls had a chance to get to know each other. I daresay we shall see her again before we go back.' George spoke with lazy good humour, and Phoebe seethed; she hadn't thought about Corina all day, and here the wretched girl was, popping up again into her head to nag her. But that was all that was said about her; Kasper was amusing as well as charming and a clever talker, and they were all laughing by the end of the meal. All the same, she was glad when they left the table. Kasper had been sitting opposite her and each time she had looked up, his dark gaze had met hers. George, sitting at the head of the table, had his eyes on her too, but she didn't know that.

Later, sitting in the drawing room over coffee, she listened to his slow, deep voice and felt she would burst with love. It would never do to give him an inkling of her feelings. In her efforts to hide them, she was alternately silent or too chatty; it was a relief when Mevrouw Thyss van Linke declared it was her bedtime, and she was able to make her own excuses and go with her. She bade Kasper a pleasant goodnight, replied suitably to his renewed invitation to visit him, offered a cheek to George and followed his mother to the door. They were leaving the room when Kasper called to her: 'I'm going very shortly, Phoebe—I won't keep George from you.'

Phoebe didn't answer, but when they reached the gallery at the top of the staircase George's mother paused.

'Do you like Kasper, my dear?'

Phoebe paused to think. 'I'm not sure that I do—only he's fascinating, isn't he? You don't mind me saying that?'

'Not in the least. I asked a question and you gave an honest answer.' She kissed Phoebe's cheek and just for a moment Phoebe thought she was

going to say more than that. 'Goodnight, my
dear.'

In her room Phoebe undressed slowly and sat
for a long time brushing her hair. She wasn't
thinking about Kasper, her head was full of
George—dear darling George, who liked her
enough to marry her, but showed no signs of
loving her. 'I must do something about that,'
muttered Phoebe as she got into bed, prepared to
stay awake until she had hit on a solution, but it
had been an eventful day; she fell asleep at once.

Mevrouw Thyss van Linke never came down to
breakfast; she and George ate it together in a small
room at the back of the hall while they discussed
what they should do with their day. 'Well,' said
Phoebe, 'it might be dull for you, but I like being
here. I mean just for a day, you know, to get my
breath.'

'Then that's what we'll do. Suppose we walk
into town? There's a quiet path across the road
and through the woods; it's a long way round but
pretty. We might see something to take back for
Mrs Thirsk . . .'

'And Nurse Wilkins and Susan.'

'Of course. You do realise that we'll have to pay
family visits before we go home? We'll space them
out so that you're not too overwhelmed.'

'I shall like that. They all come from different
parts of the country, don't they?' She added shyly:
'I liked your grandmother.'

'We'll go there first. It'll be a pleasant drive, we
can stay for lunch and have dinner on the way
back here. Tomorrow?'

She nodded. 'Oh, yes.' She filled his coffee cup.
'Your mother won't mind if we go out each day?'

'Not in the least. We're a close-knit family, you
know.'

Except for Kasper, she thought silently. She supposed they would visit him too, and she had to admit that it would be—well, interesting to meet him again. To be admired so openly was soothing to a girl who had precious little to be admired. She smiled at the thought and George said:

'You're pleased? Good. Put on some sensible shoes and we'll be off.'

The walk through the woods was delightful. The paths were sandy and they met few people; dog owners and one or two horse riders. Once at the shopping centre they had coffee and then strolled along looking, not very seriously, for suitable gifts to take back with them. It took quite some time before Phoebe saw a leather handbag which she thought was just right for Mrs Thirsk, and presently a couple of silk headscarves which would be just the thing for Susan. That left Nurse Wilkins. 'She's got her own home,' mused Phoebe, 'so china or something like that . . .' They found a Delft blue cup and saucer and plate, prettily boxed, and well satisfied, they started back home, very much at ease with each other. They reached the house far too soon, thought Phoebe, parting from George in the hall to go to her room and tidy herself for lunch, for her—although she took heart at the thought that George had enjoyed her company.

They left early the next morning, and since it was almost like a winter day Phoebe wore the Jaeger suit again. She was glad about that when she saw George's approving eyes at breakfast; it had been well worth getting up earlier than usual so that she had had time to do her face and hair really well. They set off in high good humour and drove north, at first along the motorway through

Nijkerk and Harderwijk and then to Zwolle, where
they stopped for coffee, but after that George left
the main roads and took a country road to
Steenwijk and then on to the highway to
Leeuwarden. Just short of the town he turned off
into a narrow road which in turn led to a brick
road running along the top of a dyke: the fields
were wide here, well stocked with black and white
cows wearing sacking coats, and in the distance
Phoebe caught a glimpse of water.

'Surely not the sea?' she asked.

'Lakes, all connected by canals and rivers—
we're almost there.'

Sure enough there was a cluster of houses round
a church ahead of them. George slowed to go
through its small centre and took a lane leading to
a clump of trees. A moment later he had turned
into a gravelled drive and she saw the house. Flat-
faced with a ponderous door flanked by wide
windows, it rose for two storeys with a highly
ornamental balcony running across the first floor
and rows of windows above it. Phoebe didn't say
anything; perhaps old Mevrouw Thyss van Linke
had more of her family living there with her . . .

A stern-faced woman admitted them and then
led them across the wide hall to double doors at
one side. She said something to George as she
tapped on the door and smiled at him as she
opened it. Before they went in George said,
'Phoebe, this is Marthe, who housekeeps here.' He
spoke to the woman too, and Phoebe held out a
hand and was relieved to see the housekeeper smile
again.

George's grandmother was sitting very upright
in a small armchair near a log fire, almost lost in
the huge fireplace with its great hood and coat of
arms above it. The room was large, very light by

reason of the wide high windows, and richly furnished. Phoebe, once greetings were over, found time to look around her, sitting quietly, not taking a large part in the conversation. But presently the old lady began firing questions at her, a state of affairs which lasted until they were bidden to lunch. This was eaten in another large room, its walls hung with family portraits, the dining-room table large enough to take a dozen people in comfort.

'I'll take a nap,' declared Mevrouw Thyss van Linke when they had had their coffee. 'Take Phoebe round the house, George.'

So they wandered off, peering into any number of rooms, all looking as though they were in constant use. 'Does your grandmother live here all by herself?' asked Phoebe.

'For a good deal of the time, yes. The family gather from time to time.'

'It's rather large . . .'

'The first Thyss van Linkes to live in it had ten children, and since then there have never been less than six. Grandfather was one of eight, Grandmother was the youngest of five. She married young and Grandfather was some years older than she; there's no one left now, just her, but she wouldn't dream of leaving. It's been home for too long.'

They went into the garden presently and through a small gate into the little wood beyond. It was still chilly and overcast, but as far as Phoebe was concerned it could have snowed.

They left after tea, with his grandmother's wedding gift, a silver tea service, securely packed in the boot. 'You'll do very nicely,' the old lady had said as she kissed Phoebe goodbye. 'Come again whenever you like.'

'A lovely day,' sighed Phoebe, eating a splendid dinner at the Grand Hotel Wientjes. 'George, what a large family you have!' She didn't mean to sound wistful, but he said at once: 'Enough for two of us, my dear.'

They were off again the next morning, this time to The Hague to see Tante Beatrix and Oom Charles. They lived on the outskirts of the city in a pleasant wooded area between it and Wassenaar. Another enormous house, thought Phoebe, but quite different from the one in Friesland. This one was of red brick with a good deal of ornamentation over its windows. It had a steep tiled roof and two little turrets at either end and there were steps to climb to the front door, opened by a very correct manservant. Phoebe was glad it was warm and sunny enough for her to wear a rather dashing two-piece. Six months ago she would never have dreamed of wearing anything quite so chic, but it was astonishing how quickly she was getting used to it. They were welcomed warmly, and Phoebe found that the Baroness expected her to answer all the same questions as George's grandmother. It was a relief when they were offered drinks and presently went in to lunch, a lengthy elaborate meal in an intimidating room, heavy with solid furniture, and yet more ancestors glaring from the walls. She preferred the drawing room even though it was furnished in the same heavy style.

'Well?' asked George as they drove home.

'They were awfully kind,' said Phoebe, and added carefully, 'but I liked your grandmother's house better.'

'Me too. Tante Beatrix is far too grand for me.'

That, coming from George, struck her as very amusing, although she didn't say so.

They stayed at home the next day, walking a

little, talking a great deal to George's mother, and
although they had intended to go to Groningen on
the following day, a phone call made them alter
their plans. Lena, George's cousin, was ill with 'flu
and they were advised not to go. 'So we'll go to
Rhenen instead,' suggested George. 'Kasper's still
home—I'll give him a ring.'

He was looking at Phoebe as he spoke and she
found to her annoyance that she had pinkened.
The calm of his face didn't change. 'I'll suggest
dinner, shall I?'

'Whatever you like.' Her cheeks were cooling,
thank heaven; she hoped he hadn't noticed, and
her voice was quiet and just sufficiently interested.
All the same, she didn't want to go.

They spent the next day walking in the woods
and then sitting about talking, lounging in the
comfortable chairs, listening to the radio, watching
TV, until it was time to dress for the evening.

She put on the dress George had chosen, its
silken folds falling gracefully, its magnificent belt
showing off her small waist. George would surely
be pleased that she was wearing it. She took a final
look in the mirror, caught up the wide mohair
wrap she had bought in Hilversum, and went
downstairs.

George was in the hall, his hands in his pockets,
rather remote and austere in a beautifully cut grey
suit. He looked handsome and very large and self-
assured; Phoebe thought fleetingly that he was just
as good-looking in the slacks and thin sweaters
he'd been wearing each day at home.

He turned round as she reached the bottom
stair, staring at her so intently that she said
uncertainly: 'Is there something wrong? I wore this
dress—it's the nicest of them all . . .'

'It's delightful,' he said slowly. 'You should

make a lasting impression.' Which wasn't quite the answer she had hoped for.

It wasn't a long drive and George took the side roads. It was a light pleasant evening and the country was tranquil. Phoebe felt like talking, but presently she gave up. George, always polite and beautifully mannered, wasn't in a chatty mood; she contented herself with sitting quietly, watching his hands on the wheel, weaving day dreams which, as far as she could see hadn't a hope of coming true.

Kasper's house stood well back from the road just before the small town of Rhenen. It was a fair-sized house and thatched and the garden around it, encircled by trees, was full of colour. A solid middle-aged woman opened the door to them and was brushed aside by Kasper, who greeted them with wide smiles and a further flowery speech about Phoebe's charming appearance. She wished him good evening and at the same time wished she didn't feel so awkward about his compliments but she could think of nothing to say; she had had little enough practice, after all. She glanced at George, standing beside her, wearing a bland expression which for some reason annoyed her, so that when Kasper took her hand and said, 'Come along—there's plenty of time before dinner for a drink,' she smiled at him and went down the hall and into a big room that ran the width of the house at the back. It wasn't like any of the other rooms she had seen during her stay; it was ultra-modern, sparsely furnished with curious tubular furniture, the walls hung with a flame-coloured paper. There was someone sitting on a hideous sofa—Corina.

CHAPTER SIX

PHOEBE would have paused in the doorway, but Kasper had a firm hold of her hand. 'Surprise, surprise!' he cried. 'I decided that three was the wrong number for a dinner party, so I got Corina to come along; which means that I can get to know you better, Phoebe darling, and she and George can renew their old friendship.'

Corina got up and strolled to meet them, and Phoebe was conscious of a variety of strong feelings jostling for expression. Dislike for Corina for a start, fierce jealousy because she and George were old friends—and that could cover any number of things—and fortunately for her, stronger than these, an intense satisfaction that her dress, so different from Corina's narrow-skirted, backless black satin, was a great deal more becoming. She said coolly: 'Hullo, Corina, what a surprise, how nice to see you again,' and summoned a smile which at least looked genuine. A smile which she managed to keep in place as Corina flung her arms round George's neck and kissed him.

The evening went on for ever. Dinner, in a dining room as ugly as the drawing room, all uncomfortable chairs and a glass-topped table, was a splendid meal, quite wasted on Phoebe. Even if she had stolen a march on Corina's outfit, she couldn't hope to compete with her undoubted talent for holding everyone's attention, so she smiled and laughed and said little, and she didn't look at George at all. And when Corina began to talk about people she didn't know and times long past, before Phoebe had known George, she suddenly cast good sense to the winds and encouraged Kasper's more than cousinly attentions. He was being rather silly, she thought, but at least it helped her to ignore Corina making a dead set at George, who should, she decided severely, know better.

The lengthy meal came to an end at last, and they went back to the drawing room for coffee. Phoebe, peeping at the modern clock on the overmantel, made out that it was almost ten o'clock; surely they would go soon? But George appeared to be in no hurry, nor did he seem to mind the way Kasper was monopolising her. Phoebe, made aware of strong feelings she had never experienced before, responded halfheartedly to Kasper's talk and wished they could end the evening.

Which they did some hour or so later and not entirely to her satisfaction. George, it seemed, was willing to give Corina a lift, and since she begged to sit in front by George because on the back seat she always felt car-sick, Phoebe found herself sitting lonely behind the two of them. Even Kasper's soft: 'A delightful evening, Phoebe darling, the beginning of a close friendship—England isn't so far away, you know.'

He had kissed her hand, which rather pleased her, even though she didn't much like it.

Corina talked almost without ceasing until they reached Hilversum and when George stopped the car and got out to open Phoebe's door and open the house door for her, begged her sweetly to visit her. 'There's an awful lot you should know about George,' she said lightly 'and I'm the best one to tell you.'

Phoebe went back to the car and poked her head through the window. 'I think I'd rather find out for myself,' she said gently. 'Goodnight, Corina.'

Her goodnight to George was glacial as she went past him into the house.

Corina lived with her parents in Baarn, only a few miles away. Phoebe got ready for bed and went to sit by the window until she saw the car coming up the drive again. At least George hadn't done more than drive the girl home—there hadn't been time for more than that.

She got into bed, fuming, and went to sleep at once to dream of George and Corina and Kasper, so that she woke in the early morning not sure what had been dream and what had been reality.

A condition not helped in the least by George's matter-of-fact good morning when she got down to breakfast. 'I fancy you didn't enjoy yourself overmuch at Kasper's,' he observed blandly as she poured coffee. 'I have a great many friends, Phoebe, old friends who I have known for many years—I hope that they will be your friends too when you have got to know them.'

She wasn't going to let him see that she minded; she said in a rather high voice: 'Actually, the evening was delightful, only I'm not quite used to compliments and—well, the kind of joking talk. I daresay I'll get better at it.'

'Kasper has really fallen for you—aren't you flattered?' He smiled at her across the table and she itched to throw a plate at him.

She said airily and with no truth at all: 'Yes, I suppose I am—I'm not used to it either, you see.' At his quizzical look she added hastily: 'I'm not sure that I like being flattered.'

'A good thing,' observed George placidly, 'for I

don't think I'm much good at it.' He buttered
some toast and she passed him the marmalade.
'Would you like to go anywhere today?' He
glanced up and smiled at her. 'Only three more
days, you know.'

Phoebe looked out of the window. 'Unless you
want to go somewhere . . . I'd love to just potter
around—your mother wouldn't mind?'

He gave her a pleased look. 'She'll be delighted.
She's been longing for a long gossip and tomorrow
she'll be rather occupied making sure that
everything is just as it should be for the party.' He
took the cup of coffee she was offering him. 'If
you're sure that's what you want to do, I'll drive
to Leyden to my old hospital and look up a few
men I know.'

He spoke casually, his eyes on her face.

She bent her head and busied herself with what
was on her plate.

'What a good idea,' she said brightly. 'You
trained there? It's one of the oldest medical schools
isn't it?'

Of course he wouldn't want her with him, she
would be in the way if he wanted to talk to his
former colleagues, but all the same, she felt hurt.
But wild horses wouldn't drag that from her. She
listened to him talking about Leyden, without
hearing what he was saying, her smile as bright as
her words had been.

Actually, she spent a very happy day with his
mother. While there wasn't much to say about her
own family, since she had none, Mrs Pritchard had
several dozen members to discuss, so when she had
exhausted the Dutch side, she began on the
English relations of her husband. 'All in Cumbria,'
she observed, 'but now and again they come down
to London and we have a grand get-together—and

there's a niece who's married and lives in
Cornwall—a dear girl with five—no, six children—
so unfashionable, but so happy.' She peeped at
Phoebe. 'You like children, dear?'

'Very much.' Phoebe had been expecting that
and her voice was composed. 'I expect that's
because there haven't been any in my family for
such a long time.'

'Ah well,' Mrs Pritchard sounded pleased with
herself, 'that's something that can be remedied,
and how fortunate that George has the means to
care for half-a-dozen children.'

Phoebe mustered a smile and agreed.

George was back shortly after they had had tea
and the rest of the evening passed pleasantly
enough, what with his account of how he had
spent his day and Mrs Pritchard's plans for the
next day's party.

'Will there be a lot of people coming?' asked
Phoebe, 'and do we dress up?'

'About thirty or so, and yes, I think we might
dress up, Phoebe. There will be a buffet supper
and dancing; it's a chance for even more family
and our friends to meet you.'

It was their last day. Phoebe got up and looked
out of the window with real regret; she had loved
every minute of her stay and she had got to know
a good deal more about George too. She dressed
and went down to breakfast, to find him already
there, and when he suggested a walk through the
woods she agreed happily.

'You've liked it here?' he wanted to know as
they took a sandy path away from the house.

'Oh, yes, George—I love it. And I do so like
your mother.'

'And she finds you exactly the kind of daughter-
in-law she wanted.'

'Does she? Does she really? Well, I'm glad. You know, you seem quite a different person here, George—I mean, I wouldn't have guessed the half of this, just knowing you in Woolpit.'

'That's why I wanted us to come here. In a couple of days I'll be a village G.P. again.' He smiled wonderfully at her and tucked her arm under his. 'And you'll be a G.P.'s wife, answering the phone and the door and taking messages.'

'I shall like that.' She beamed at him, 'I hope your mother comes to stay with us soon.'

'She will.'

They walked on in a companionable silence until Phoebe asked: 'Have you known Corina a very long time?'

'Oh, years and years.' His voice was dry. 'You find her pretty?'

'Very—and very attractive.' There was a faint question in her voice which he didn't answer, so she changed the subject hastily. 'That dress we bought in the Hague—the one with the long bodice and the chiffon skirt—would that be too grand for this evening?'

'Certainly not. I should think it would do admirably—you are, after all, the belle of the ball.'

'No, I'll never be that,' she said soberly, 'although it's kind of you to say so.'

All the same, when the evening came and she put the dress on, she had to admit, even to her critical eye, that it really was something. She hadn't dared to query its price, but it was undoubtedly haute couture; the dropped bodice, apricot silk embroidered with silver thread, merged into a swirl of silk chiffon skirts, and when she had dressed her pale brown hair high and applied an extra special make-up, she couldn't help but be pleased with her appearance. She was preparing to

go down to the drawing room when there was a
tap on the door and George came in. He closed the
door behind him and stood looking at her. 'Very
nice,' he commented, studying her at his leisure,
and then he strolled towards her. He took at once
a hand out of a pocket and she saw the shimmer of
pearls. 'Will you wear these? My father's mother's
pearls—he left them to me for my bride, and
tonight seems a fitting occasion on which to wear
them.'

It was a three-stranded pearl choker with a
diamond clasp, and Phoebe took it in her hands,
touching the pearls gently. 'They're beautiful,' she
whispered. 'You're sure you want me to have
them?'

He smiled. 'Are you not my bride?' And when
she looked at him uncertainly, 'And I want you to
have them, my dear.'

He fastened them and she turned to look at
them in the mirror. They were exactly right with
the dress. She turned back, one hand on the pearls.
'Thank you, George—it's the most beautiful thing
I've ever seen . . .'

He bent his head and kissed her lightly. 'I'm
glad you like them. Shall we go down?'

Mrs Pritchard was already in the drawing room,
its furniture set against the walls so that later on
anyone who wished could dance. She was wearing
black velvet and a discreet sprinkling of diamonds,
and Phoebe was on the point of exclaiming how
very nice she looked when Mrs Pritchard
forestalled her. 'Phoebe—but how enchanting, and
the pearls are just right. That's an exquisite dress,
my dear. George, aren't you proud of your wife?'

'I've always been that—I'm utterly charmed as
well.'

Phoebe blushed and wished with all her heart

that he had really meant that. Of course, he was
being kind, putting her at her ease, making her feel
beautiful when she wasn't. She said shyly: 'Thank
you, Mrs Pritchard, you look lovely.'

Mrs Pritchard twinkled. 'Mother of the bride-
groom,' she laughed. 'I always promised myself I
would deck myself out in black velvet and
diamonds—so dignified and suitable.' She smiled
at her son and Phoebe looked at him too. He was
handsome and distinguished and she wanted to say
so, but she couldn't get the words out. His eyes
held hers and she might have gone on gazing at
him for ever if Mrs Pritchard hadn't observed
matter-of-factly: 'There are sandwiches in the
sitting room—supper will be late and we'll be
famished . . .'

She led the way across the hall and Phoebe and
George followed her. Halfway across the hall he
stopped, caught her by the hand and kissed her.
She stared up at him wide-eyed. 'Oh, why did you
do that?'

'One day I'll tell you.'

It was exasperating when his mother paused
ahead of them and turned round, and disappointing that George didn't look in the least
put out.

The guests began to arrive presently. Phoebe
had met a good many of them already and she
began to enjoy herself, sometimes with George
beside her, sometimes the centre of his friendly
family. She felt they liked her and she blossomed
out under their kindly chatter. She was standing
talking to a circle of the younger guests and a
sprinkling of cousins when Corina and her parents
came in—they were late, but she guessed that it
was deliberate on Corina's part so that she might
make an entry. Which she certainly did. She

looked magnificent in vivid emerald green, a slinky
tube of a dress, slit up the side, an enormous bow
on one hip making her appear even slimmer than
she was. She greeted Mrs Pritchard perfunctorily,
leaving her parents to do so in a more leisurely
way, and crossed the room to where George was
standing with a group of guests. Phoebe couldn't
hear what she said, and anyway it was in Dutch,
but she laid a hand on his arm and smiled up at
him in a way to make Phoebe seethe with rage, a
rage by no means mitigated by George's smile and
laughing rejoinder. Phoebe turned a shoulder and
pretended that she hadn't noticed, and when
Corina and George appeared at her elbow
managed to look both delighted and surprised.

'How nice to see you, Corina,' she uttered
insincerely, 'and what a gorgeous dress.'

Corina's eyes took in every inch of Phoebe. 'I
see you've wrested the pearls from George. I
always rather fancied them, though they are not
quite my style.'

Spiteful cat, thought Phoebe, and felt jealousy
turn a sharp knife deep inside her—was she
implying that George had once upon a time
offered them to her? Aloud she said in her pleasant
voice: 'You don't need pearls, Corina, you're
pretty enough without.' She smiled around the
circle of faces. 'What about supper? Shall we see
what there is to eat? I believe we're going to dance
presently . . .'

She felt her hand taken from someone behind
her and turned to see Kasper smiling down at her.
'Hullo, beautiful cousin.' He nodded at the others.
'Did I hear you mention food? I'm famished, let's
attack the buffet.'

He urged everyone towards the dining room,
still holding Phoebe's hand, laughing and joking,

calling over his shoulder: 'See you later, Corina—
and George.'

Perhaps, thought Phoebe uneasily, she and
George would have been expected to go in to
supper together, but it was too late to do anything
about that now. She found herself surrounded
with a laughing cheerful crowd, with Kasper still
close, his hand on her arm.

'You look terrific,' he whispered, 'and I've never
seen Corina look so vulgar.' He got her a plate of
food and all of them sat down at one of the tables
arranged round the room. 'To our very own fairy
on the Christmas tree,' cried Kasper, and raised
his glass to her.

It wasn't George, but just to be admired by
someone, even if she didn't like him at all, was
soothing to her pride. And Kasper, give him his
due, was expert at keeping up the party spirit.
Presently they all went back to the drawing room,
where someone had already started the record
player, and Phoebe found herself swept on to the
floor. Kasper danced well and she, although she
had never had much chance to dance, was
instinctively good at it, and when the music
changed to pop, she fell to twisting and twirling as
though she had done it all her life.

'I say,' said Kasper, 'you're pretty good—is this
another of your hidden talents, Phoebe?'

'I didn't know I had any.' She swung round and
found herself face to face with George, who
whisked her away to the edge of the room where it
wasn't so crowded. 'Having fun?' he wanted to
know.

'Oh, yes.' She made her voice enthusiastic; it was
already breathless because she was with him. 'It's a
wonderful party,' she added. 'Isn't it?'

She glanced at him and then quickly away, so

that she didn't see his thoughtful eyes on her face.
'I'm glad you're enjoying it. You'll find life dull
when we get home.'

She didn't look at him. 'Oh, George, no! It will
be lovely.' She paused, remembering how he had
smiled at Corina, and added deliberately and
recklessly: 'I shall miss Kasper, though, he's such
fun.'

'Then we must ask him to visit us,' said George
at his most placid. 'Be sure and do so before he
leaves.'

She had already regretted it: 'We can always
write.'

He had danced her round the room and come to
halt by the French windows. 'Oh, that's not the
same.' He turned towards the dancers and lifted a
hand to Kasper, dancing past with Corina.

'Phoebe wants to have you to stay,' he said
easily. 'Fix up something between you.' He
beamed warmly at them both and danced off with
Corina.

'Well, well,' murmured Kasper. 'If I didn't know
you were newlyweds I might be getting ideas!'

Phoebe pinned a bright smile to a stricken face.
'Pooh, what nonsense—George would like you to
come and see us too. Are you a busy person? I
mean, what do you do?'

'Absolutely nothing,' declared Kasper. 'I'm the
black sheep of the family, we all have far too much
money, but I'm the only one who idles away my
life, spending it.' He smiled beguilingly. 'I'll come
when you want me to, little cousin.'

'Well, it's lovely in England in the early
summer—June . . .'

'June it shall be. Shall I be bored with the rustic
life?'

She looked surprised. 'I don't know. You see,

I'm never bored, and I don't think George is either. But there's some lovely country round and about Woolpit, and you can always drive up to London if you can't bear it any more.'

'It's a deal. I'll come at the end of June—I'll bring the car so that we can explore a bit while George has his handsome nose to his stethoscope or whatever.'

He bent and kissed her cheek. 'A bargain sealed,' he explained at her look of surprise. 'I can't see George—probably in a quiet corner explaining things to Corina. Let's dance.'

'What do you mean?' asked Phoebe in a quiet little voice.

'Oh, nothing sinister, darling. The dear girl had her claws into him the moment she'd left school, and she's not one to take no for an answer.'

And if that wasn't a word of warning, what was? thought Phoebe.

She changed partners presently, and it was some time before she found herself dancing with George once more.

'Fixed things up with Kasper?' he wanted to know placidly.

'Yes. The end of June. George, you and Corina ... were you ever engaged? I mean, she seems— that is, she's a very old friend ...'

His voice became even more placid. 'Oh, a very old friend. But no, we were never engaged. Why do you ask?'

'Oh, no reason ...' She tried to sound nonchalant. 'She's very pretty.'

'Very.' They danced in silence then, and Phoebe, to her shame, had the hardest job in the world not to burst into tears, a circumstance which gave her heightened colour and a very bright pair of eyes.

People began to leave round about one o'clock.

She kissed aunts and uncles and family friends goodbye, exchanged wishes to visit, accepted invitations and gave them, and finally found no one left but Kasper, the van Renkels and Corina and a rather tart old aunt who lived nearby in Hilversum. Phoebe helped her on with a vast number of shawls, topped with a fur coat, while the old lady mulled over her evening.

'Very pleasant,' she observed in her stilted, quite perfect English. 'You will be an asset to the family, my dear. George has taken his time to find himself a wife, but I see he has chosen wisely.' She shot a beady-eyed look across the hall, to where Corina was talking to George and Kasper. 'Such a relief!'

George joined them then to take her out to her car and stow her carefully into the back seat, and by the time he came back the van Renkels had said their goodbyes and Kasper was preparing to leave too.

They all went through the door together and George went with them, and Phoebe and Mrs Pritchard went to the sitting room and sat down. Ulco had set a tray of coffee and a plate of sandwiches on a small table and Mrs Pritchard went to pour out. They had almost finished their first cups when George joined them.

'Kasper having a last-minute chat?' asked Mrs Pritchard.

George accepted a cup of coffee and took a sandwich. 'No—Corina, nattering on about this and that.'

He sat down opposite Phoebe and she took care not to look at him, giving her whole attention to her coffee.

'I thought her dress was most spectacular,' remarked Mrs Pritchard in a carefully expressionless voice. 'Has she got designs on Kasper?'

'They don't like each other.' George sounded faintly bored.

'Oh, really? Then I wonder for whose benefit she wore that very vulgar dress?' Mrs Pritchard didn't wait for an answer, but went on: 'I thought your cousin Sibilla looked charming.' She turned to Phoebe. 'That was the dark-haired girl who came with my sister, dear, such a sweet girl . . .'

They sat talking for some time until Mrs Pritchard glanced at the great Friesian wall clock and exclaimed at the time. 'Good gracious, it's past two o'clock! I shall have my breakfast in bed—and you do the same if you want to, my dear. Have you done your packing?'

Phoebe shook her head. 'But that won't take long and we don't go until the afternoon, but I think I'll come to bed too.'

And when George got up she offered him a cool cheek for his kiss and wished him an equally cool goodnight.

Just before they left the next day an enormous bunch of red roses was delivered. The card that came with it read: 'To my favourite cousin, *tot ziens*.'

George put the flowers carefully on the back seat. He didn't appear to mind about them in the least, a fact which Phoebe found very disappointing. If only the silly man knew that I'd rather have a weed from the garden as long as he'd picked it and given it to me, she thought.

Hard on the thought came the much more disquieting one that perhaps he had sent red roses to Corina.

Their journey home was uneventful. Mrs Thirsk was waiting for them with a nicely laid table and a late supper ready. She accepted her presents with pleasure, told George that his post was on his desk in the study, and assured Phoebe that there were no worries since she had been away. Then she had departed to dish up supper while Beauty dashed between the study and the sitting room, beside herself with delight.

Half an hour later, sitting opposite George, eating Mrs Thirsk's delicious omelette, Phoebe felt as though she had just wakened from a dream. Only it hadn't been a dream; there were red roses, arranged in a great glass vase, to prove her wrong.

The evening had gone by the time they had finished. They sat for a while over their coffee but presently George went back to his study and she, after a word with Mrs Thirsk, went up to her room and unpacked. Hanging her lovely clothes in the enormous clothes closet, she wondered when she would wear them again; they weren't really suitable for Woolpit and she didn't think that George was a man to spend his few free evenings living it up in London. She lay for a long time in a very hot bath, pondering the events of the last few days or so. She had liked his mother—more, she was fond of her, and she liked his family, although she wasn't quite sure about Kasper. Corina was the only cloud in her sky and unfortunately she was a large one, looming dangerously. Perhaps George was in love with her; she wasn't sure of that, his face gave nothing of his feelings away, and Corina would have made him an unsuitable wife. Even if he loved her desperately, he would have admitted that; anyone less likely to make a village doctor's wife would be hard to find. Whereas she . . . 'Most suitable,' she said out loud, 'able to answer the phone, talk to patients, do a little bandaging on the side and probably sit on a variety of village committees . . .' She licked away a tear. 'And happy to wear simple sensible clothes.'

She lay there until the water cooled around her, dried herself, slapped cream on to her flushed face, and got into bed. She had been there for some time, still wakeful, when she heard George's quiet footfall crossing the landing. It was only then that she fell into a troubled sleep.

She didn't look her best in the morning; her eyes were a little puffy and she was too pale, but when George, already at breakfast, remarked on her looks with some concern, she brushed it aside. 'It was a long day, yesterday,' she pointed out. 'Would you like me to help in the surgery this morning?'

He shook his head. 'Take Beauty for a walk, if you like. Andrew will be over presently—there are one or two patients we must check over together. See you later for coffee, perhaps.'

So Phoebe went for a long walk with an ecstatic Beauty, to get back home just as Mrs Thirsk was carrying in the coffee tray. She had coffee with the two men, sitting between them while they discussed their work. Now and again they remembered that she was there, and Andrew asked her how she had enjoyed herself in Holland, and George wanted to know if she had enjoyed her walk, but she suspected that she was surplus to their needs at the moment, and presently, with a murmured excuse, slipped away. It wouldn't be like that all the time, she told herself bracingly.

And it wasn't. At breakfast the next morning she was invited to put on a white overall and go along to the waiting room. Dr Pritchard was back; the word had gone round the village, and patients who had put off paying a visit to the surgery because he was away had been ringing up, making appointments. 'If you'd take names and get their cards out for me,' suggested George, 'it would save a great deal of my time.'

Phoebe was delighted; at last she was being of some use. The waiting room was filling up fast when she got there, although the surgery wasn't open for another ten minutes or so. Indeed, George was in the garden with Beauty, she could see him as she stood at the filing cabinet. She had the time to put old Mrs Owen's notes on his desk before he went into his surgery through the garden door. And after her there was Billy Pearce, with one of his regular sore throats and his rather bad-tempered mum, and Mrs Platt from the shop with what she called a nasty sharp pain inside. Just where inside was she was reluctant to say, although she informed the occupants of the waiting room that it was something cruel and she hadn't had a wink of sleep. She was almost immediately eclipsed by Mrs Foster with an even worse pain in her leg. Phoebe, searching for their cards and notes, made soothing noises, ushered them in one by one and made appointments for those who would need to come again. It was quite a busy morning and well past eleven o'clock before she poked her head round the surgery door.

'That's the last,' she told George cheerfully. 'I've taken two calls; one from Mappit's Farm and one from a Mr Westcott, both in bed with what sounds like bad chests, though neither of them were very clear about symptoms.'

He looked up from his writing. 'That will be the Mappit boy—he's an asthmatic—and Mr Westcott has chronic bronchitis.' He leafed through the notebook on his desk. 'I've another four or five calls to make—would you like to come with me?'

Phoebe's eyes sparkled. 'Oh, please, George. Coffee first?'

And when he nodded, she went along to the kitchen and then raced upstairs to re-do her face and find a cardigan.

Mappit's Farm was several miles out of Woolpit, but they didn't talk much; she guessed that George's mind was on his patients, so she kept quiet, content to sit beside him. Really this was much better than the parties and outings they had had in Holland. Those had been fun too, of course, but here at home, they were doing something together.

He wasn't long at the farm, although most of the other calls took longer. She sat in the car, not impatient, dreaming of the perfect future she longed for and which was so unlikely. But she couldn't help but dream, all the same.

They took Beauty for a walk after lunch and came back to one of Mrs Thirsk's splendid teas, eaten hurriedly on George's part because he had a call to make before they had even finished. Phoebe took the tray out to the kitchen, had a pleasant gossip with Mrs Thirsk and went to tidy herself. By the time she was downstairs it was almost time for evening surgery and George wasn't back. The waiting room already held several patients; she found their cards and put them ready on the surgery desk, passed the time of day with this patient and that and went away to take another phone call—an agitated voice this time, asking if the doctor could call. 'Grandma's a very nasty colour,' said the voice, 'I don't like the look of her.'

It took a few moments to get the patient's whereabouts and another minute or two to reassure the caller. Luckily the address was one of the cottages at the end of the village street, and as she put down the receiver she heard the car at the door.

George, primed with her details, drove off at once and she went back to the waiting room to explain the delay. It seemed that Grandma was a well-known member of the community, and an interesting discussion as to her chances of survival kept everyone interested until George got back.

The evening surgery went smoothly enough after that. It was while she was tidying the waiting room when the last patient had gone that Phoebe asked: 'Was she all right, the old lady?'

George turned off his desk light and got up. 'Indigestion,' he said. 'She's eighty-eight and as sound as a bell, but she will indulge her fancy for pickled onions. What's for supper? I'm famished!'

A lovely day, thought Phoebe, curled up in bed a few hours later. If they could all be like that, life would be—if not quite perfect, then getting on that way; no Corina, no Kasper . . . Holland was a long way away. She thought to herself sleepily and she had George alone here. She was dozing off when the tiresome thought that perhaps he might find life with her a little dull flashed through her mind. She tried to remember what they had talked about during the evening. Nothing very interesting—indeed, he had read the papers for a good deal of the time while she sat opposite him, knitting. Compared with Corina in her lovely clothes, laughing her tinkling laugh, she was deadly dull. As from tomorrow, she would change into a pretty dress each evening and do her best to make witty conversation so that he would laugh at her as he had laughed at Corina. She closed her eyes again; perhaps tomorrow would be as nice a day as today had been.

CHAPTER SEVEN

TOMORROW, Phoebe was delighted to discover, was every bit as good as the previous day had been, and so were the succeeding days. And as the days lengthened and the weather settled into a promise of summer, they began to get invitations to visit George's friends. He seemed to have any number of them, scattered round the countryside, making their evening drives an added pleasure; more than that for Phoebe, it was heaven to sit beside George as he drove, listening to his desultory talk about his day, asking her opinion of this and that, laughing with her over some amusing incident. And his friends were nice. She had been scared before the first invitation, but afterwards she had to admit to herself that she had enjoyed every minute of it. George's friends had been youngish, with children and a comfortable untidy home and they had made her welcome and accepted her. Then after that she looked forward to their other visits, wearing the dresses George had chosen for her in the Hague and taking great care about her hair and make-up.

'We'll have to give a dinner party ourselves,' observed George, driving back through the still light evening. 'Shall we start with four? The Mansells and the Prices—they get on well together, and the Gregorys and the Normans a little later on.' He glanced sideways at her. 'It had better be on a Saturday or Sunday evening, we've got more chance of being free then.'

Phoebe said worriedly: 'I've never ... I'm not sure I'll know what to do.'

'Just be you, Phoebe—they all like you, they won't be looking for faults, you know. You and Mrs Thirsk put your heads together and see what you can cook up between you. It's my weekend off in ten days—shall we decide on Saturday and see if the others are free then?'

'Yes, all right. Do you want me to write to Maureen and Leslie?' She added: 'Leslie's such a super cook . . .'

He laughed. 'A good reason for you and Mrs Thirsk to outshine her!'

A remark which made Phoebe decide to take a cookery book with her to bed each night; not that she would have to do the actual cooking, she thought comfortably. As things turned out, she was wrong. Having decided on a menu with Mrs Thirsk, the flowers, the table linen, the silver, Phoebe, relieved that everything was settled, occupied her days happily enough; as well as helping George in the surgery when he needed her, there was the garden, presided over by a taciturn old man who, once he had got used to the idea, raised no objection to her pottering alongside him, flowers to be arranged, shopping to do, occasional coffee mornings to attend, and the accounts to do—her days were nicely filled and she was happy. It was the day before the dinner party that Mrs Thirsk went down with 'flu. Sitting up in her bed, in an old-fashioned white nightie and a substantial bedjacket, she peered at Phoebe's anxious face from fever-bright eyes.

'You'll need to start today, Mrs Pritchard; it's all written down and everything's in the fridge. Do the watercress soup first. The lamb's coming this morning—Jim will have prepared the crown roast, the veg will be easy enough—new potatoes, like we said. As for the pavlova, that's easy . . .'

Phoebe agreed faintly; she had eaten pavlova when George had taken her out, but how to make it was a mystery she must solve. Mrs Thirsk was in no state to bother with such details. She went to the kitchen and looked over the contents of the fridge. At least she could get the soup ready. She peeled potatoes, cut them up and boiled them, added almost all the watercress, black-peppered it carefully and hopefully pushed the lot into the *mouli-légumes*. To her delight it came out looking like soup; she poured it carefully into a bowl and put it into the fridge. She would only have to reheat it at the last moment, add the cream and the watercress sprigs, and the first course was dealt with.

Quite cook-a-hoop as she was, it seemed the right moment to tackle the pavlova; the filling she could do just before the dinner party, but the meringue would keep fresh in the freezer. She followed the recipe painstakingly, getting rather hot and bothered before finally getting it into the oven. It was rather a pity that Susan should choose that moment to cut her finger. Not a bad cut, but it needed attention and, Susan being Susan, needed a cup of tea so that she could pull herself together again. What with one thing and another, Phoebe forgot the meringue. The ultra-crisp remnants which she took from the oven some time later were consigned to the dustbin. She would have another go after lunch, she decided. Now it was time to get a meal for George, who would be home from his morning rounds at any minute. Omelette, she decided, and a salad, and thank heaven there was a treacle tart in the fridge. She managed to have everything on the table as George swept into the house, although she hadn't had any time to tidy herself.

George threw her a quick glance. 'Busy?' he wanted to know cheerfully. 'How's Mrs Thirsk? I must see her presently.'

Phoebe observed that the housekeeper was feeling rotten and hadn't fancied anything for lunch but some soup. It would be too much to hope, she thought wistfully, that George might make some sympathetic remark about her busy morning. She stifled a wish to tell him how clever she'd been about the watercress soup and what a mess she'd made of the meringue for the pavlova, and she assured him cheerfully that she had no problems about their dinner party.

So, after lunch, with Susan enlisted to clear away lunch and wash up, Phoebe had another go at the pavlova, this time with success, mainly because she stayed glued to the kitchen for an hour until the meringue was exactly right. But at least she filled in the time mashing bananas and brandy to fill it later on, and when that was done getting down to making the saffron rice, a slow business with its half a dozen ingredients and all the stirring, but at last it was finished. She added the petits pois, the butter, the nuts and the little bits of apple and got out the crown of lamb and began to cover the top of each rib with foil, much encouraged by Susan's ohs and ahs of admiration.

She had to stop then and get the tea. George had gone into Stowmarket, but he would be back around four o'clock. There was no surgery, it being a Saturday evening, although there was always the chance that he might be called out. Phoebe sent Susan home for her own tea and gave her strict instructions to be back by half-past seven, since she was to provide background help in the kitchen and wait at table, and then she took up a tray to the housekeeper. Mrs Thirsk was feeling a little better. Phoebe listened thankfully to last-minute instructions and went downstairs in time to welcome George.

'Had a pleasant afternoon?' he enquired, coming into the kitchen to carry in the tea tray.

'Oh, very.' Phoebe's voice sounded a little hollow, although she smiled cheerfully.

She enjoyed arranging the table. The cloth was a shining starched damask, the silver shone and so did the crystal glasses—George had beautiful things in his home. She had arranged a flower centrepiece in a low bowl and decided against candles in favour of the delicate chandelier hanging above the table. By the time she had everything to her satisfaction it was time to dress. She showered and put on one of the dresses George had chosen—pale green with a wide satin belt—and then hurried over her face and hair; it was time to put the crown of lamb in the oven.

She wasn't sure how she managed to be in the drawing room a minute or two ahead of their first guests. She was flushed from the heat of the Aga and her hair had come a little loose, and George gave her a long look as she came into the room. His placid, 'You look nice', more than made up for her hectic day.

On the whole, the evening went well; true the foil had somehow fallen off the tops of the ribs and they had got charred, but she had covered them with the cutlet frills and prayed that no one would take them off, and they hadn't. And even if the saffron rice didn't taste quite as delicious as it would have done if Mrs Thirsk had made it, it looked very nice.

Maureen and Leslie both declared that she was a splendid cook and they drank her health too. 'You must have been hard at it all day without

Mrs Thirsk to give you a hand,' observed Leslie
kindly, and Phoebe felt a pleasant pang of
satisfaction at the surprise on George's face.

It was after everyone had gone, and Susan,
replete with the remains of the dinner party, her
evening's earnings clutched in a hand, had gone
home too, that George said: 'That was a splendid
effort, Phoebe, you must be tired to death. Go on
up to bed, we can clear up in the morning.'

Phoebe had had a quick look round the dining
room. The table was just as they had left it and
when she peeped into the kitchen, there seemed to
be a mountain of saucepans and dishes. Susan had
stacked everything neatly before she had gone, but
they would have to be washed.

She said brightly: 'I'm not a bit tired. I'll just
clear the dining room; it'll be far worse if it's left
until the morning.'

They began on the table, and it was almost
cleared when the phone went.

George put down a pile of plates. 'I'll go,' he
said, and glanced at the clock. It was well after
midnight.

'The Bissett baby—sounds like croup.' He was
already on his way to the study to fetch his bag.
'Don't wait up, my dear.'

Phoebe gave a tired snort as he closed the door
quietly behind him. It was likely that she would be
a long time clearing away the mess. She set to
work on the dining room and when she had
cleared it, put the kettle on, made a pot of tea, let
Beauty out into the garden, kicked off her very
expensive kid shoes and put on an apron.

The tea revived her and she set to, feeling more
cheerful, going slowly because the silver had to be
rubbed with Mrs Thirsk's special cloths and the
glasses, hundreds of them, it seemed to her, needed

precise polishing. She put them away in the big glass-fronted cupboard in the dining room, laid the silver carefully in the baize lined box, then started on the plates. It was striking one o'clock when she began on the saucepans, and half an hour after that when George came quietly back into the house. She heard him go into his study and then lock the street door and tread down the hall and into the kitchen. He said softly: 'Good God, my poor dear,' and took the tea towel from her and put his arms round her, and she buried her face in his waistcoat, wanting very badly to burst into tears. If he kissed her, she wasn't sure what she'd do ... but he didn't, only patted her shoulder and said kindly: 'Now off with you—I'll finish this little lot,' and when she would have protested, 'No, not a word—bed for the cook, my girl.'

There didn't seem to be anything to say to that. Phoebe murmured goodnight and did as she had been told, and once in bed had a nice refreshing weep before she finally slept.

They laughed about it over breakfast in the morning, and it wasn't until that meal was over that Phoebe, making some remark about the Bissett baby, discovered that George had been out again at four o'clock in the morning, this time to drive the small sufferer and his mother to Stowmarket hospital. 'But you've had no sleep!' she cried worriedly. 'Thank heaven it's Sunday.'

'You don't want to go anywhere?'

'No. It's a lovely day, we can sit in the garden and read the papers. After church,' she added hastily. George, she had quickly discovered, was very firm about going to church on a Sunday. She enjoyed going down the village street to the morning service, and liked the sound of George's

deep voice booming away at the hymns and the
way he sat, listening to every word of John
Matthews' sermon. Afterwards they went back
home and had coffee and then took Beauty for a
walk before Phoebe took a tray up to Mrs Thirsk,
now almost herself once more. When she got back
to the kitchen it was to find that George had put
things haphazard on to a tray and carried it out to
the garden, and they had a picnic in a rough-and-
ready fashion, reading the Sunday newspapers
while they ate. Afterwards George went to sleep,
lying out on the smooth lawn, his firm mouth very
slightly open and uttering the faintest of snores.
Phoebe sat and watched him, her face alight with
love, but presently she got up silently and carried
everything back indoors. The washing up would
wait. She went outside again and sat down close to
George with Beauty's head in her lap. Just for a
little while she was utterly content.

Mrs Pritchard phoned later in the day; she
would be coming to England for a couple of
months, probably in August. 'And I'll come and
stay with you for a few days if you'll have me,' she
told them, 'before I go to Grantchester. I can't
come sooner. Your grandmother isn't very well—
nothing serious, the doctor says, but she's asked
me to stay in Holland until she feels herself again.'

They spent the evening discussing her visit and
exchanging views on the Sunday papers, and
Phoebe cooked a mixed grill, not quite Cordon
Bleu, but George ate it, which was all she wanted.

Mrs Thirsk was so much better in the morning
that she had to be restrained from getting up and
going down to her kitchen. 'After lunch,' said
Phoebe persuasively. 'There's nothing much to do.
Susan's here seeing to the house, and I'll get a cold
lunch for us; the doctor's got to go to Cambridge

directly after his visits and won't be back until tea time at least.'

'I'll cook supper,' declared Mrs Thirsk obstinately.

'Oh, please do,' said Phoebe. 'You've no idea how much we've missed you.'

A remark which caused the housekeeper's rather stern features to relax into a pleased smile.

A week went by, a very pleasant one, although at the end of it Phoebe had to admit to herself that nothing in the least exciting had happened to enliven it. Indeed, she had been busy almost all day, what with helping in the surgery, pottering round in the house and garden and taking Beauty for her walk. She had taken over all the shopping now, too, and the accounts, so that she had little time in which to sit and laze. As far as she was concerned she would be happy—well, almost happy—to go on like that for ever. The summer stretched ahead of her and anything could happen.

But not quite what she dreamed of so constantly. It was after a busy Monday morning surgery, soon after George had driven off to the first of his visits, that a black Mercedes nosed its way down the village street and came to a halt outside the house. Phoebe, walking up the main street from the butcher's shop, her basket over her arm, wondered idly whose car it could be—someone too late for surgery, perhaps? She hurried her footsteps and arrived at her front door just as the front door of the car opened and Kasper got out, and after him, Corina.

Phoebe stood, her mouth slightly open, unable to believe her own eyes. Kasper's cheerful, 'Hullo, little cousin,' only made it worse. She looked from him to Corina, a glowing picture in a trouser suit and a camisole top. She found her voice then.

'What a surprise! I expect George forgot to let me know . . .'

'He doesn't know—we decided we would give you a real surprise. We wanted a holiday, and where else to go but to our so English George and his charming wife?'

Phoebe shifted her basket to the other arm, one part of her mind reminding her that she would have to go back to the butcher's and get more steak. 'Well, do come in—George is doing his morning visits, but he'll be home for lunch—you'll stay, won't you?'

Corina let out a peal of laughter. 'Stay? Of course we'll stay—there's room enough for the two of us, I imagine, and we hadn't planned to go anywhere else.' She looked around her. 'I must say it's quiet—a real English village.' She turned to Kasper. 'Bring in the cases, Kasper—I'm dying for coffee!'

Phoebe, bereft of words, opened the door and led the way in. 'If you will go into the sitting room,' she suggested, 'I'll get Mrs Thirsk to get the coffee.' She went along to the kitchen, trying not to notice the suitcases that Kasper was bringing into the hall—enough for a month's stay, she decided, her heart in her shoes.

In the kitchen Mrs Thirsk was podding the young broad beans Susan had brought with her. She took a look at Phoebe's face and said at once: 'What's wrong, Mrs Pritchard? What's the matter?'

'We've got unexpected guests, Mrs Thirsk—the doctor's cousin from Holland and—and an old friend. They want to stay. Could we possibly have coffee?' She put her shopping basket on the table. 'I'll go back for more steak presently, and perhaps Susan could do some more vegetables. The two rooms in the back wing have beds made up, don't they? They'd better have those.'

Phoebe sounded so unlike her usual self that the housekeeper said quickly: 'Don't you worry about a little thing, Mrs Pritchard, the rooms are quite ready. Susan can slip down to the butcher presently—there'll be four for lunch? You see to them and I'll be along with the coffee in five minutes.'

She was as good as her word. Phoebe, sitting uneasily exchanging nothings with Corina and listening to Kasper's lighthearted remarks about their journey, welcomed the diversion, while Mrs Thirsk took her time setting the tray on a side table while her sharp eyes took in the visitors. She had responded distantly but suitably to Phoebe's introductions, and when she had gone Corina said: 'Bad-tempered, is she not?'

Phoebe was quick to defend her trusted helper. 'Good heavens, no—what makes you say that? She's marvellous and runs the house so beautifully, and she's a splendid cook. George and I think of her as a friend as well as a housekeeper.'

Corina threw up her hands in mock dismay. 'I seem to have upset you. It was only my impression. I have not seen her before—last time I came she was on holiday.'

Kasper sat drinking his coffee and smiling to himself. Phoebe, glancing at him, wondered what she had found attractive about him in Holland. Here he was thoroughly out of place, so for that matter was Corina; so disrupting the even tenor of their lives.

Corina put her cup down. 'I'd like a shower before lunch. Where am I to sleep? Last time I had a big room at the side.'

'Come upstairs and I'll show you—if Kasper would bring up your case?'

He laughed. 'You mean cases! Corina never travels without at least a month's supply of clothes.'

Phoebe led the way upstairs. 'Oh, God—at the back of the house,' observed Corina crossly. 'Poky rooms, and I suppose I can't have a bathroom to myself?'

'Afraid not,' said Phoebe politely. 'It's just next door to your room, though, and only you and Kasper will be using it.'

'There's another bathroom, though, as well as the one I suppose you and George use.'

Phoebe heard the lies tripping off her tongue and she, a truthful girl, felt no shame. 'Sorry, but the plumbing needs attention—it's not in use for the moment.' She had gone into the bedroom with Corina and cast a quick eye round to see that everything was just so. 'We lunch at one, so come just when you're ready.'

She went back downstairs, glad to be away from Corina's ill humour, to discover Kasper sitting at his ease, a glass of sherry at his elbow.

'Taken you by surprise, haven't we, Phoebe? Corina has these sudden fancies and nothing will shake her out of them or make her change her mind—besides, I must confess that I wanted to see you in your role of housewife.' He grinned. 'Perhaps it's nearer the truth to say that I wanted to see you, full stop.'

Phoebe eyed him coldly. 'Do help yourself to a drink,' she said crisply. 'I must see about lunch.'

She went into the dining room and started to lay the table, just as she always did. She didn't hurry about it because she wanted to be in the hall when George got back. She glanced out of the window

and saw the Mercedes still there, and hurried back
to Kasper.

'Will you move your car; there's a lane a few
yards along the road—you can put it there for the
moment. We leave the front free for George.'

'If you say so, darling Phoebe.' He drank the
rest of his sherry and went out of the door, and
Mrs Thirsk came into the dining-room and stood
watching him with Phoebe beside her.

'Will it be a long stay?' she asked softly.

'I don't know.' Phoebe felt a childish desire to
burst into tears. 'I daresay they'll tell the doctor.
We'd better ask Susan if she would pop up each
evening and give you a hand with the washing up
and tidying the kitchen. It won't be too much
work for you, Mrs Thirsk? I'll help as much as I
can, and perhaps they won't stay for more than a
day or two.' She broke off. 'Here's the doctor.'

She got to the door as George opened it, but
before she could say anything she saw him look
over her shoulder and heard Corina's voice from
the stairs. 'Surprise, surprise, darling—I thought
you'd like it if I came to cheer you up for a bit.'

George's expression, his usual expression of
placid good humour, didn't alter. He paused just
long enough to drop a brief kiss on Phoebe's cheek
and then he went past her into the hall.

'Who brought you?' he asked blandly.

'Kasper—I made him. He's here somewhere.'

'I asked him to put the car in the lane,'
explained Phoebe in a wooden voice, and watched
Corina fling her arms around George's neck and
kiss him. The girl had changed into a stunning
outfit—white linen with a vivid green sweater, her
make-up was faultless and so was her hair.
Phoebe, without the chance to do things to her
face and hair, felt positively dowdy.

George took Corina's arms from his neck. 'Well, now you're here, come and have a drink.' He glanced at Phoebe and smiled faintly. 'Lunch?'

'In about ten minutes. I was just going to see how Mrs Thirsk was getting on.'

'Really George,' drawled Corina, 'Phoebe is almost too good to be true.'

He agreed blandly and turned to meet Kasper, strolling into the house, just as though he owned it, thought Phoebe furiously, as she went to find Mrs Thirsk.

That good lady wisely said nothing; lunch was ready and she had found time to prepare shrimp cocktails. 'I'll take them in now, Mrs Pritchard, and we'll have the rhubarb tart and cream for afters. I'll make a creme caramel for this evening— they'll be here for dinner?'

'It seems as though they will, Mrs Thirsk—I'll let you know as soon as I can.'

'Well, don't you fret yourself, ma'am, but we'd better do something more than the omelette we'd planned—will you and the doctor be going to that concert?'

Phoebe had forgotten that. 'Oh, lord—perhaps we can get two more tickets. We must go because the doctor promised—it's for the League of Friends and we were specially invited.'

She went back to the drawing room, accepted a glass of sherry from George and started a conversation with Kasper, since Corina was deep in conversation with George, and since they were speaking Dutch, it made it difficult to join in. She sat listening to Kasper's amusing talk, not hearing above half of it, since she was trying to understand what Corina was saying, and she was rescued with Mrs Thirsk's announcement that lunch was on the table. It was during that meal that George observed mildly: 'Corina and Kasper plan to stay with us for at least a week, Phoebe.'

She hoped that her horror at the news didn't show on her face. She said: 'How nice—we must think up a few trips while they're here. The country is so pretty . . .'

Corina gave her tinkling laugh. 'Oh, country—how boring! All right for you, Phoebe darling—you're a country girl at heart, aren't you? I want to do some shopping and visit a restaurant or two.'

'Well, we can start with this evening.' George's voice was so placid as usual. 'Phoebe and I have an invitation to a concert which we have no wish to break. I'll get two more tickets.'

'What kind of concert?' said Kasper idly.

'Orchestral and piano.'

Corina looked horrified. 'Piano?—No pop? Isn't there a disco somewhere?'

'Probably. I've never enquired,' said George, still placid. 'But I'll make enquiries and you and Kasper can go along and dance the night away.'

Corina pouted prettily. 'That isn't what I meant. Why don't you come too, darling George?'

He turned a bland face to her. 'I prefer my home—besides, I'm a busy man and I enjoy our quiet evenings.'

Corina's eyes sparkled. 'Oh, we'll have to change all that, won't we, Kasper?'

'We can always try! What about you, Phoebe?'

Phoebe said quietly, not looking at George, 'I like doing whatever George likes doing.' She smiled brightly round the table. 'Shall we have coffee in the drawing room?' Only then did she look at George. 'You're not in a hurry, George?'

She saw him shake his head. 'A couple of calls, but I can spare half an hour still. I'll see about those tickets.'

While they drank their coffee Corina kept the conversation firmly in her hands, talking about people Phoebe didn't know, recalling occasions when she and George had been dancing or dining. If only he'd mind, thought Phoebe. If she had to go on smiling much longer her face would crack. It was quite a relief when George got up to go, refusing quite firmly to take Corina with him. 'You'll be here when I get back,' he said casually, 'and the only person I take with me is Phoebe—she's a nurse, you see, and gives me a hand if I need one.'

Corina professed herself bored the moment George had driven away. 'I'll unpack,' she declared, 'and have a nap—someone can bring me a cup of tea at about four o'clock.'

'I'll let you know when it's teatime,' said Phoebe. 'We have it in the sitting room.'

Corina flounced off, leaving Kasper lolling in his chair, still smiling. Phoebe got up. 'I've got things to do; there are some pleasant walks if you'd like to go out—I'll see you at teatime.'

His eyes widened with laughter. 'I do believe you don't like having us here!'

She stood in front of him and gave him a straight look. 'Since you ask, no, I don't, but you're George's guests, so I shall do my best to see that you enjoy yourselves.'

'Well, well, my little cousin has a sharp tongue! Let's hope George doesn't come under its sting.'

'George doesn't need to.'

In the kitchen Mrs Thirsk was tackling a mountain of dirty dishes. 'Susan will be back soon,' she explained, 'when she's had her dinner—she wanted to go home for it—she's a good girl.'

'Indeed she is. I'll dry, and while I'm doing that we can plan the meals for tomorrow. Our guests

will breakfast with us, Mrs Thirsk—probably
Juffrouw van Renkel will ask for her breakfast in
bed, but I'm afraid, as they arrived unexpectedly,
they'll have to fit in with the doctor's mealtimes.
I'll not have him inconvenienced.'

'Indeed not, ma'am.' Mrs Thirsk sounding
approving. 'How about a nice piece of fish for
tomorrow? There's that trout in the freezer—new
potatoes and peas and a nice sauce. And an
upside-down pudding for afters, the doctor likes
them.'

'That sounds splendid. What about this evening?
We'll have to eat at seven o'clock sharp—the
concert is at half-past eight.'

'Tomato soup,' said Mrs Thirsk promptly,
'lamb chops and a green salad, ice cream for
afters. Would that do?'

'Admirably. Do you want any extra help, Mrs
Thirsk? A week is a long time . . .'

The housekeeper stole a look at Phoebe's
unhappy face. 'Gone in a flash,' she said bracingly,
'specially if you take one day at a time. Me and
Susan will manage very well, the lady and
gentleman can look after themselves when you're
in the surgery with the doctor—I daresay they'll go
for a walk. They're not . . .?' she paused
expectantly.

'No, I don't think so, Mrs Thirsk, but I really
don't know. They've known each other a long
time, though.'

Mrs Thirsk made a strange muffled snorting
sound and muttered something Phoebe didn't hear
and decided not to notice. She didn't blame Mrs
Thirsk for being put out.

In bed that night Phoebe came to the unhappy
conclusion that the evening hadn't been a success.
Corina had kept them waiting for dinner and had

appeared, a vision in vivid pink, to keep them
waiting still further because she simply had to have
a drink before they sat down. Then she refused the
lamb chops and asked for an omelette, so that by
the time they were ready to leave, it was late. It
was fortunate that they only had to go to Bury St
Edmunds, no distance at all; all the same, they
barely had time to take their seats. Phoebe sat up
in bed and pummelled her pillows in a sudden
rage. Corina had contrived to hang back, so that
Phoebe found herself with Kasper beside her, and
Corina between the two men. She sat, not hearing
any of the concert, reflecting that she might just as
well not have gone. It had helped a bit when the
concert was over, for George had taken her arm
and let the other two go on ahead.

'You enjoyed the concert?' he wanted to know.

'Oh, very much—they were all splendid, weren't
they? I liked the concerto.'

'What are we to do with our guests tomorrow?
Have you any ideas?' They were walking very
slowly and a throng of people separated them
from Corina and Kasper.

'Well, no. Would they like to go for a country
walk?'

He let out a rumble of laughter. 'Corina in four-
inch heels? Very unlikely. Besides, I've several
babies coming for their triple injections and I
could do with your help—they'd better go off on
their own in the morning.' He smiled at her so
kindly that she had felt tears crowd her throat. She
smiled back at him, suddenly almost happy
again. Only it was shortlived; Corina had turned
back impatiently and slipped an arm into
George's, wanting to know if there was somewhere
lively where they could dance for an hour.

He had said no very decidedly. 'You forget that

I'm a working man,' he had reminded her. His answer had consoled Phoebe; it was a small consolation, but it helped.

She got up heavy-eyed after a troubled night's sleep and went downstairs to find George already at the table. His, 'Good morning,' was brisk, and as soon as she had sat down he went back to his post. Presently he looked up. 'What about Kasper and Corina?' he asked.

'They had early morning tea and they know breakfast is at half-past seven.'

He leaned back in his chair. He said with a slow smile: 'You know, my dear, I fancy you have depths that I haven't yet plumbed.'

Phoebe didn't answer that but poured coffee, buttered toast and began on her breakfast. Ten minutes later Kasper appeared. He wasn't at his best in the morning, she decided; his face looked puffy and there was no sign at all of all that charm. She made polite enquiries as to his night's sleep, put his toast near, poured his coffee and offered him a boiled egg.

'I looked in on Corina,' he observed grumpily. 'She's still in bed.'

'Too bad,' said Phoebe tartly, and refused to meet George's surprised look. 'I'll be in the surgery, Kasper, for the next hour or so. We usually have coffee after that, but if you two want to go out would you let Mrs Thirsk know, then she'll know what to do about lunch.' She smiled pleasantly. 'And now, if you'll excuse me, I must just go and see Mrs Thirsk in the kitchen . . .'

When she got back, George had gone to the surgery and Kasper was still at the table smoking. 'They'll be coming to clear the table,' she told him sweetly. 'The papers are in the sitting room.'

Kasper laughed. 'And Corina's breakfast?'

'I'm sorry, but you must see that we have to keep to a strict timetable unless George is on holiday. I daresay she'll be down by the time we have coffee.'

She whisked away, donned her overall and went along to the waiting room, where she dealt with her usual calm with the patients, handed forms, wrote up cards, undressed a couple of babies and helped old Mrs Oakes to unwrap the layers of clothing she always wore, winter and summer, so that George could take a look at her painfully wheezing chest.

Surgery took longer than usual and then there was the clearing up to do while George sat at his desk, filling in forms and making notes. He didn't have anything to say and Phoebe, already regretting her sharpness at breakfast, held her tongue. Presently they went together back to the sitting room, where pacing up and down like a beautiful caged tiger they found Corina. Kasper was lounging in a chair, reading the papers.

'Well, I must say——' Corina began, and broke into a torrent of Dutch, ignoring Phoebe.

George answered her in English. 'I daresay you didn't quite understand, when you decided to visit us, that I have a working day just like anyone else who earns his living, and since Phoebe helps me, there's precious little time to do anything else.' He sounded matter-of-fact and added: 'Here's coffee—why not go for a stroll through the village? Phoebe has to shop, I daresay, and get the lunch. Perhaps this afternoon . . .'

'I'll come with you when you do your visits.' Corina was smiling again.

'No.' He looked at Phoebe. 'Will you pour the coffee, my dear?'

The day passed uneasily. Corina refused to go

for a drive with Kasper but sat about the house saying nothing, only when George came back did she become animated. A wretched day, Phoebe decided, getting thankfully into her bed.

She did her best the next day, still conscious that she had been less than hospitable to her unwelcome guests. She persuaded Kasper to drive them to Cambridge, showed them as much of the city as possible, took them to lunch at the University Arms and possessed herself in patience while Corina went in and out of various shops, only to return empty-handed.

'I must be taken to London,' she declared crossly.

Phoebe did not comment.

They took a disastrous picnic into the country the next day, and it rained, and the following day Phoebe, unable to think of anything else to do, suggested going to a film in Cambridge. It was all very well for George, she thought vexedly, he was hardly ever home, and the only time Corina was animated and smiling was when he got back in the evenings.

She sat after dinner, trying not to notice how Corina was charming him while she herself lent an inattentive ear to Kasper. The week was nearly up and no one had said a word about leaving. For two pins I'll leave myself, she thought, and heard George say carelessly: 'By the way, we've got a measles epidemic on our hands. Nasty thing, measles, and easily caught. It's not too bad with children, but there are two mothers with it already, and it hits hard with adults.'

Corina lounging gracefully on the sofa sat up smartly. 'I've not had measles. Is it spots? Is it dangerous George?'

'Well, hardly fatal, but the rash is nasty and one

is liable to get chest infections and bad eyes, hair falling out and so on.'

'I will not stay here with this measles, however much you beg me. Kasper, you will drive me to London tomorrow.' She darted a look at George. 'These patients—do they come to the surgery with this measles?'

He shrugged. 'Bound to—they don't always recognise that they have the symptoms.'

'We shall go after breakfast.' Phoebe, listening and not saying a word, had never heard such good news in all her life.

CHAPTER EIGHT

THE rest of the evening was taken up with discussions; patient and goodnatured on George's part, amused on Kasper's and pettish on Corina's. Phoebe contributed little to the talk, as a good deal of it was in Dutch and she felt sure that anything she might have to say would bear little weight with Corina. She offered more coffee, undertook to see that both her guests would be called betimes and asked diffidently if she could help Corina to pack.

Corina had refused. 'There's no room for two in that poky bedroom,' she observed waspishly, and had turned her attention on George once more.

'You must come up to London,' she urged. 'We haven't had any fun—I want to dance and have supper at a decent restaurant.'

George had smiled gently. 'Kasper dances far better than I do, and he knows all the best restaurants. Besides, we can't get away.'

Corina slid a malicious glance towards Phoebe. 'Tied by the leg?' she asked, and laughed.

Watching the Mercedes driving away the next morning, Phoebe thought that she had never been so happy—a happiness mitigated by an uneasy feeling that she had been less than a perfect hostess. But then Corina had needled her unmercifully and it had been hard to take her lighthearted jibes meekly. She went back into the house and met Mrs Thirsk coming from the dining room. 'Nice to be back on our own again, Mrs Pritchard,' she observed. 'How about a cheese soufflé and asparagus for lunch? and Susan's brought some strawberries . . .'

'Oh, lovely, Mrs Thirsk!' Phoebe danced upstairs and began to strip the beds; the day, already bright and warm, promised to be golden indeed.

She realised, when George rang the surgery bell for her to give him a hand, that she had hardly spoken to him while Corina and Kasper had been there—not alone, that was; they had had no chance, either one or other of their guests had been there and she had had to spend a good deal of time behind the scenes, organising meals and tidying rooms. She put on her overall and went through the waiting room to the surgery, to find George there with a weeping mother and a small screaming boy.

He said unhurriedly: 'If you would hold Ronnie, my dear, while I take a look for Kopek's spots.'

Phoebe smiled at the young woman and lifted the kicking small boy off her lap and set him on her own. Despite the fact that she was small she was strong; she held him firmly, his arms imprisoned against her, while George prised open his reluctant mouth and inserted the spatula.

'Yes, it's measles, I'm afraid, Mrs Watt. Take him home and put him to bed—and take care not to let him go near the baby. I'll be along later with some medicine and then I'll take a look at the baby at the same time.'

When Mrs Watt had led a tearful Ronnie away, he said: 'That's the third this morning—nine cases since Thursday. Thank heaven most of the children here have had their jabs. Send in the next patient, will you, Phoebe?'

Surgery finished, they spent twenty minutes or so, he at his desk, she clearing away whatever had been used, and tidying the waiting room. Finished, she said, 'Coffee when you're ready, George,' and went back to the sitting room where Mrs Thirsk had already put the coffee tray.

'It seems quiet without our visitors,' observed George as Phoebe poured out.

'Yes, and dull for you.' She hadn't meant to say that, but somehow it had popped out.

'Dull?' His voice was silky.

'Well, Corina is ... well, she's so alive and amusing and pretty to look at, and Kasper is amusing too.'

'You think so? I had the impression from time to time that you thought the opposite.'

She put down her cup with a hand that shook just a little. 'Oh well, I expect that was because I was thinking about meals and—and that sort of thing.'

'I don't seem to have seen much of you,' he said mildly.

Phoebe felt a rare ill temper taking possession of her. 'I don't suppose you did,' she snapped. 'I expect if I were an experienced hostess I could have taken everything in my stride, but I'm not; you have no idea—and why should it bother you anyway? What a problem it is to think of meals, and the extra housework—beds to make and rooms to dust, and making coffee at all hours; and all the extra washing up and having to sit there, talking nothings while you know you should be laying the table or making a salad!'

George put down his coffee cup and she was furious to see that he was laughing. 'My poor Phoebe, and I quite thought you would enjoy some young company. I'm afraid I never thought about all the chores.'

It was really too much! She got to her feet and

bounced out of the room and ran upstairs. There were still beds to make and perhaps if she had something to do she would feel better. He shouldn't have laughed, she told herself, and allowed the held-back tears to trickle down her cheeks.

Over lunch, again calm and freshly made-up, she enquired politely about the measles, mentioned an invitation to dine with some friends of his in a nearby village and remarked on the quite beautiful day.

To all of which George replied with a bland calm which she suspected hid amusement. They had almost finished when he said casually: 'How about an evening in town? We could meet Kasper and Corina and have dinner and dance. A small reward for all your hard work during the last week, Phoebe.'

The rage which she had so carefully mastered came racing back, almost choking her. The wretched pair had only been gone a few hours and here he was suggesting that they should race after them—probably he and Corina had arranged it; hadn't the girl been nagging at him to take her dancing?

'I can think of nothing more enjoyable,' she declared mendaciously. 'When do we go?'

George looked at her from under half shut lids, his eyes very intent. 'Saturday? We can arrange to meet somewhere—the Savoy, perhaps?'

'Very nice,' said Phoebe in a wooden voice. 'Will you be in for tea? I thought I'd go and see how old Mrs Down's getting on—she's worried about her cat.' At his enquiring look: 'He's off his food, if he's ill I'll ring the vet and get him to take a look.'

'You're happy, Phoebe?' asked George suddenly.

'Me?' She smiled in his general direction without meeting his eyes. 'Yes, thank you, George.'

'Why thank me?' he asked blandly. 'I hardly feel I deserve thanks. You don't feel that ... You don't regret marrying me?'

Phoebe was thankful that she could answer that with perfect truth. 'Heavens, no! I love living here, it's a lovely village and everyone is so kind—it's so nice to feel wanted.'

George was looking at her and she frowned a little because it had been a silly thing to say. 'People tell me about their children and grannies and things like that, and then there's the surgery most days, and the house. I never have a dull moment.'

'You're content?'

It was on the tip of her tongue to shout no, she wasn't anything of the sort, she would never be until he loved her as much as she loved him, and that wasn't in the least likely. 'Quite.' That sounded bald; she added: 'And I'm fond of your mother.'

There didn't seem any point in adding to that, so she muttered: 'Mrs Down ...' and smiled briefly as she went.

It would be splendid, she thought as she made her way to Mrs Down's cottage, if she could catch the measles. Then George could go to London on his own.

She had never felt better; she put on the dress she had worn for the party in Holland, took pains with her hair and face and joined George in the hall ready for their drive to London. She had prayed all day that some emergency would arise which would keep him busy; not that she wished harm to anyone, and it was George's weekend off anyway, so even an emergency would have been

transferred to one of the other local doctors, but a
suspected appendix or a fractured femur in the
village would have been providential—held him up
for long enough to make it too late to drive to
London. However, the village remained healthy to
a man, and Phoebe got into the car, feeling guilty
because she had hoped otherwise.

It was a beautiful evening and the roads were
quiet. They made good time and parked at the
Savoy exactly on time. They hadn't talked much
on the way, casual remarks about nothing in
particular, the easy chat of old friends. She had
hoped that George might have made some remark
about her appearance, but beyond a casual:
'That's a pretty dress,' he had said nothing.
Phoebe wondered unhappily if he had even looked
at her long enough to notice that she had altered
her hairstyle. I'll tint it red, she thought crossly,
and wear it in spikes—not that he'd notice.

Kasper and Corina were in the bar, and the first
thing Corina said was: 'Hullo, darlings—Phoebe,
you're wearing that dress again—of course you
don't have much chance to dress up, do you?' She
gave Phoebe a sugary sweet smile and kissed
George, which made it easier for Phoebe to put up
with Kasper's lingering salute.

She smiled back at Corina and said gently:
'Well, of course, if we had a really big date, I'd get
something new.' She allowed her gaze to linger on
Corina's vivid pink sheath. 'Haven't you been
shopping yet?' she asked gently. 'Of course you
haven't really had time.' She smiled at Kasper. 'I'd
love a drink—gin and tonic, please.'

It was a drink she had never sampled; she
disliked the smell of gin for a start, it reminded her
of petrol, but so many people drank it there must
be something about it . . .

When it came she sipped it. It was as disgusting as she had imagined it would be, but since George was watching her, a half-smile on his face, she took another sip and murmured: 'Very nice,' for his benefit.

They sat a while over their drinks before going through to the restaurant, and Phoebe, determined not to enjoy herself, found it difficult not to feel a thrill of pleasure at its grandeur. If she had been alone with George she would have exclaimed with delight, but since the other three took their surroundings as a matter of course, she did the same, prudently choosing a cold mousse to start with and thankfully, at George's suggestion, agreeing to Supreme de Turbotin Walwska to follow. Sherry trifle seemed a safe bet after that, a delicious sweet which she ate with pleasure, ignoring Corina's impatient pecking and complaints about the food. Phoebe, watching her push away the *mille-feuille* she had chosen, wondered what on earth she had thought of the far simpler meals she had had while she had been staying with them. No wonder the girl was as thin as a beanpole, and what a waste of good food and money. They had been drinking champagne. Now Corina demanded another bottle and pushed back her chair. 'Come on, George, I want to dance.'

Phoebe didn't look at him as he got up and followed Corina towards the dance floor. She hoped that one or other of them, even both, would twist an ankle, then felt horrified at her thought.

'Want to dance?' asked Kasper.

'Not yet—I'd like some coffee, please.'

He ordered it and sat back, looking at her and smiling. She wished he didn't smile so much. 'How long are you staying in London?' she asked.

'Oh, a few days, I suppose. It depends on how

much shopping Corina wants to do. Or how long we can put up with each other's company.'

Phoebe turned surprised eyes on him. 'But you're old friends . . .'

'So I'm told. I endeavour to remember it.' She poured the coffee and handed him a cup. 'Are you happy, Phoebe?' he asked.

She busied herself with the sugar. 'Yes,' she said steadily, 'very!' She smiled briefly at him. 'Why do you ask?'

He shrugged. 'George took a long time to settle down, I suppose I thought that he was happy enough leading a bachelor existence; after all, there are compensations.'

She said quietly: 'I expect there are—you could say that about any state in life, I suppose. Do you come here a lot? It's magnificent, isn't it?'

'I've been put in my place,' Kasper laughed softly. 'I do wonder what goes on behind that calm face of yours, Phoebe.'

She didn't answer that but put down her coffee cup. 'I'd like to dance,' she told him.

The dance floor was fairly crowded, but she saw George and Corina at once. George wasn't talking but Corina was, looking up into his placid face, laughing a little. Phoebe looked away and concentrated on her dancing.

When they got back to their table George and Corina were there. George was drinking coffee, but Corina was still at the champagne. She waved and giggled as they sat down. 'What do you say to going on to a nightclub? I know George wants to take me, only he says you aren't keen, Phoebe. I don't suppose you are—I daresay you've never been to one, have you? All the same, I want to go. Kasper can drive you back to that village of yours.'

'You've had too much champagne,' said George levelly. 'You've no idea what you're saying—and a good thing too, because you're being offensive. I've no intention of taking you anywhere; I'm going to dance with my wife and then we shall drive back to "that village of ours". Kasper knows all the best night spots; he'll take you.'

'I don't want to go with Kasper.'

'Give her some coffee,' suggested George, and got up. 'Phoebe, shall we dance?'

Phoebe allowed herself a few blissful moments with George's arms around her, his elegant shirtfront against her nose. He danced well without effort and with no fussy mannerisms, and she floated round with him, not speaking.

'Enjoying yourself, Phoebe?'

What a nice voice he had, she thought, deep and rather slow and warm.

'Oh, yes, fabulous, isn't it? I've never been anywhere like this before.' She made herself look up at his quiet face. 'George, if you want to go on to a night club I don't mind.' She added apologetically, 'I've never been to one,' and when he didn't answer at once: 'I wouldn't like to spoil the evening for everyone.'

'As far as I'm concerned, it's already spoilt, Phoebe.'

There was no answer to that one. They danced in silence while she tried to think of something to say, and at the same time wonder exactly what he had meant. Had she spoilt the evening? She had done her best, but she hadn't really improved since that disastrous party with Basil; she was still shy and uncertain and she had been rude to Corina. The beastly girl had been rude to her, but apparently if one was pretty and amusing enough one could get away with anything.

The dance ended and when they went back to their table Kasper and Corina had their heads together, laughing softly and whispering. They looked up and smiled widely. 'We're going on to a night spot,' said Kasper. 'Corina has decided that if she can't have George she'll make do with me.'

George stood looking at them both, smiled a little and said: 'Enjoy yourselves. Let us know when you're going back to Holland.' He kissed Corina's cheek. 'A delightful evening.' He shook Kasper's hand and stood patiently while the two girls pecked the air by each other's cheeks and Kasper kissed Phoebe with unnecessary deliberation. They parted company at the table, leaving George to pay the bill, turning to wave carelessly as they left the restaurant.

Phoebe preceded George a few moments later after he had paused to speak to the restaurant manager. George, she reflected with satisfaction, was the kind of man who merited such attention; he made no fuss, never raised his voice, and yet he commanded attention without effort.

She got into the car beside him and sat quietly while he drove through the quiet streets. The theatres had disgorged their audiences long since and there weren't many people about. They were past Tower Hamlets, making for the Chelmsford Road, before George spoke.

'It's a pity those two don't marry each other,' he observed placidly. 'They have a lot in common. Of course, they've known each other for such a long time, so there's no novelty—besides, Kasper's more than half in love with you.'

Phoebe, who had been curled up cosily, sat up straight. 'What do you mean? What nonsense— why, I might just as well say you're more than half in love with Corina!'

She could have bitten off her treacherous tongue. She added lamely: 'It's just as absurd.' And when he didn't say anything, her tongue took over again. 'She's more than half in love with you.'

She could detect nothing more than amusement in his voice. 'Corina is more than half in love with every man she knows.' She heard him chuckle. 'I should feel flattered that the idea should even enter your head.'

Phoebe muttered something. He was treating it as a joke, but it was no joke to her. She would have liked to have given vent to her rage and fright and misery, but she couldn't, not without him wondering why she, usually so composed, should exhibit such strong feelings.

'Nothing to say, Phoebe?' he asked silkily.

She summoned a hollow laugh. 'It was a silly idea, wasn't it? It must be all the excitement of the evening.' Anxious to get the conversation on to a more impersonal note, she went on: 'I had no idea that the Savoy was so grand. Have you been there very often?'

'Off and on, yes. But now the practice is so large that I've rather given up the bright lights.'

'You miss them?'

'Not any more, although I must confess that in the right company they still hold some attraction.'

Here we go again, thought Phoebe; it was as if Corina was sitting between them in the car. If only the girl would go back to Holland and stay there! No, Holland wasn't far enough—Australia would do, or the wilds of Brazil. She was a challenge, of course, but Phoebe wondered, just for a moment, if she would have married George if she had known about her. Only for a moment, though. Just to stay married to George she was prepared to take on a dozen Corinas.

They were clear of Chelmsford now and the country was quiet under the moon. 'It's going to be a fine day tomorrow,' said George quietly. 'Let's spend it at home doing nothing.'

She agreed with such fervour that he glanced at her. Her profile, clear and visible in the moonlight, looked sad despite her words. He dropped a hand on to her knee. 'You looked very pretty this evening,' he told her.

Her 'thank you' was a whisper, while she wondered if he meant it or if it was a kindly and probably remorseful attempt to cheer her up.

'I meant that,' he said, and stopped the car. Phoebe was quite unprepared for his sudden hard kiss, but she had no need to say anything, because he drove on again at once, and when he spoke next it was a mundane remark about taking Beauty to the vet the next week.

They went together into the quiet house. The hall looked welcoming with the shaded lamp on the wall table, and in the sitting room Mrs Thirsk had left a tray with cups and a thermos jug of coffee. George glanced at his watch. 'It's late, perhaps you're tired, but we've seen very little of each other lately. Shall we have a cup of coffee and talk?'

Phoebe wasn't in the least tired, and perhaps if they could sit together for an hour and talk they might get back to their first friendly footing—only of course it could never be quite that again for her, but George need never find out. She wondered how she would have felt about Corina if she hadn't been in love with him.

She curled up in an easy chair and kicked off her slippers while he poured their coffee, then went to sit opposite her with Beauty pressed up against his legs.

'Let's hope there won't be any more measles cases until Monday morning,' he smiled at her. 'That's wishful thinking, of course. At the least the children who haven't had jabs are turning up for them. It needs a mild epidemic to remind the mums.'

'None of the children are bad, are they?'

'No, although I hope none of the toddlers get it. We must ask Susan if she's had them, she's the eldest of four. How is she settling down with Mrs Thirsk?'

'They get on famously.' Phoebe was glad to have such a mundane subject to discuss, for she suddenly felt shy of George, sitting there, elegant in his dinner jacket and somehow remote too. He had wanted to talk, but surely not about measles? Was he going to tell her that their marriage wasn't turning out quite as he had hoped? She dismissed this idea at once, they hadn't been married long enough to give it a fair trial. Perhaps he wanted to explain about Corina, but she didn't think it could be that either, since he had no reason to explain anything. They hadn't pretended that they had loved each other when they married, so he wasn't being disloyal; it was just bad luck that Corina should have come back into their lives . . .

She was searching round for something else to talk about when George said blandly: 'You'd like to know about Corina, wouldn't you?'

Phoebe said a little wildly: 'No, I wouldn't,' and at the same time wanted to deny that. 'I'm not in the least bit interested. Anyway, it's all so obvious. I mean, she's an old friend, isn't she? You must enjoy meeting her again.' Her tongue ran on quite ridiculously. 'She's so pretty and . . . it's all such a waste of time, isn't it? and I think I'm tired after all.'

She whipped off the chair and skidded across the room on her shoeless feet and ran upstairs at a great rate, just as though she expected George to run after her. Only he didn't.

And the next morning at breakfast he behaved just as though they hadn't parted so awkwardly. He made pleasant conversation about this and that, and when they got up from table observed that he would take Beauty for a walk before joining her in the garden. Phoebe longed to go with him, but she knew that he wouldn't ask her to—besides, she had made a complete idiot of herself. The chance of them getting back to their old friendly footing seemed more remote than ever, and all because she had been a fool.

She pottered round the house after he had gone, getting in Mrs Thirsk's way until she finally fetched her knitting and went into the garden. It was a glorious morning and the sun was brilliant. She perched herself on the edge of a garden chair and tried to look unconcerned and relaxed—not very successfully, though, because the knitting became confused and a jumble of stitches, and she was busy unpicking it when George returned.

He had Beauty with him and the Sunday papers were under one arm, as he stretched himself out in a lounger beside her.

Phoebe, rewinding wool at a great rate, said: 'I'll get the coffee.'

'Mrs Thirsk's bringing it, she saw me coming out here.' He closed his eyes and Beauty spread herself on the grass between them. They must make a cosily domestic group, thought Phoebe, and saw that Mrs Thirsk thought just that as she crossed the lawn towards them.

'That's right,' said that lady, 'you enjoy a nice sit-down—there's nothing like an hour or two with the Sunday papers, I always say.' She beamed at Phoebe. 'It's a nice cold chicken salad for supper, ma'am.'

'Oh, thank you, Mrs Thirsk,' Phoebe strove to look the part of a contented housewife. 'And if your nephew comes early do for heaven's sake leave the washing up, won't you? It's such a lovely day that you mustn't miss any of the rest of it.'

Mrs Thirsk went on smiling. 'Oh, I'll get finished on time,' she said comfortably, 'and I've got my key. It's little Jane's birthday, so I daresay I'll be back a bit late.'

George opened one eye. 'There's a small parcel for little Jane on the hall table—and go easy on the Guinness, Mrs Thirsk.'

She chuckled. 'Now, Doctor, you know as well as I do that I hate the stuff.'

He opened the other eye. 'That's why I do tell you to go easy with it.'

Phoebe poured the coffee and presently he went to sleep, lying on his back, looking, thought Phoebe severely, far too handsome for his own good. She went on doggedly with her knitting and presently gave way to the warmth of the sun and closed her eyes. When she opened them, half an hour or more later, it was to find George sitting up, looking at her over the top of his paper.

'Oh, lord, was I snoring?' she demanded. She didn't wait for him to reply but picked up her knitting and raced along a row, concentrating fiercely.

'No. I was watching you sleeping.' He smiled with such charm that her heart stopped and then beat so fast that she had no breath. 'It's the first time,' he pointed out. 'You're always wide awake and bent on filling the shining hour with as many jobs as you can fill in.'

She steadied her breath. 'You find that annoying? You see, I've always had things to do, and now that I don't need to do them, I feel guilty ...' She added, anxious to seem keen to please, 'I'll change, really I will.'

'Don't you do that, my dear. You're very nice as you are.' He rolled over and picked up the paper again. 'By the way, I took your slippers upstairs and left them in your room.'

Phoebe blushed. 'Oh, thank you. I—I'm sorry about last night.'

George glanced quickly at her hot face and turned back to his reading. 'So am I, but for entirely different reasons, I imagine.'

She would have liked to have asked what those reasons were, but he was absorbed in the sports page. She went back to her knitting; perhaps things weren't as bad as she had thought. Corina had come and gone and probably they wouldn't see her again for a long time, time enough for her to get closer to George. She wasn't sure how to do that, because she had no sexy little tricks and she wasn't anything special to look at. She could only rely on being there, as well dressed as possible, a good companion and hostess to his friends, handy in the surgery when she was needed, and ready to listen to him when he wanted to talk.

The rest of the day passed in peaceful leisure. Mrs Thirsk, wearing her best summer hat, departed with her nephew to drive to Bury St Edmunds, and the old house was quiet. They sat in the garden again, reading and lying in the sun doing nothing, not even talking, and presently Phoebe went into the house and made the tea and George carried the tray outside again, cucumber sandwiches, cut paper thin as only Mrs Thirsk could cut them, china tea and a walnut cake.

'As far as I'm concerned this particular Sunday afternoon can go on for ever,' observed George. 'I'd better take Beauty for her walk before church.'

He didn't suggest that Phoebe should go with him and she didn't ask, although she had hoped that he might since they seemed to have become good friends again. While he was gone, she set the supper table, made sure that the meal was ready for them when they got back, then went upstairs to shower and put on something other than the sleeveless cotton dress she had worn all day. She heard George come in and go to his room while she was still getting ready, donning a pretty patterned silky dress and a plain straw hat, gloves and a clutch bag. She surveyed her person with some satisfaction when she was ready; she looked every inch a doctor's wife, and it was satisfying too to see her own opinion reflected in George's glance when she joined him in the hall. She did her best to listen to the sermon, but it was hard not to be gratified by the glances of approval cast in her direction from the surrounding pews.

George went to his study after supper and she cleared away, set the table for breakfast, then went to the kitchen to wash up and leave everything tidy for the morning, and since George showed no signs of joining her she tapped on the study door, put her neat head round it, wished him goodnight and went upstairs. She could always read in bed.

The waiting room was full the next morning. Phoebe had taken a quick peep after they had left the breakfast table, taken the plates and silver out to the kitchen and got into her overall. George had gone into the garden with Beauty before going to his surgery and she started on the patients' cards. Mr Maggs was back again, puffing and blowing and a nasty colour with it. Phoebe sympathised with him because he looked a bit lonely and frightened—as well he might be; a widower living on his own and no family to keep an eye on him. She found his card, assured him that he would be first in, and passed on to Miss Stokes, complaining loudly of her rheumatics and telling everyone who would listen that the world was coming to something when a body couldn't have the doctor to visit her decently at home.

'Well, if you were unable to come,' Phoebe pointed out reasonably, 'the doctor would be round at once.'

There was a murmur of approval from everyone else there. George was liked; he was dependable and kind and very clever as well. Phoebe, hearing various voices raised in his praise, beamed with pride.

She sent Mr Maggs in when George buzzed and went unhurriedly from chair to chair; small boys with cuts and bruises, two little girls with their mothers, both suspiciously spotty, a teenage boy from one of the farms with a septic finger, the butcher's wife with a burned hand … It was a couple of hours before the last of them went into the surgery. Phoebe rushed around now she was on her own tidying magazines, straightening chairs, opening the windows. She would see to George's surgery when they had had coffee and then dash upstairs and make the beds before nipping down to the stores. She was waiting, her usual calm self, by the time George came into the sitting room.

'I can't think how I managed before you married me,' he told her in his calm way. 'You did a splendid job this morning, Phoebe.' He took his coffee cup and sat down in his big chair. 'If it gets too much for you, let me know and I'll get a nurse-receptionist.'

She said 'No!' so fiercely that he stared at her, so that she went pink and stammered a little. 'What I mean is, I enjoy the work and I've got almost nothing to do in the house with Mrs Thirsk and now Susan . . .' She added rather desperately: 'I don't want anything to change.'

George's face didn't alter at all, but she had the impression that he was angry—perhaps disappointed was more like it, and she wondered why, then dismissed the thought as imagination on her part, because he went on to talk placidly about his mother's visit later in the summer.

For the rest of the day she hardly saw him. It was one of those days when half the village required his services, even as they were finishing their supper he was called out to one of the outlying farms, and although he wasn't long away he had no sooner got indoors than the phone rang and he went to his study to answer it. He left the door open and Phoebe, leafing through a magazine, couldn't help but hear that he spoke in Dutch. She went to the kitchen to speak to Mrs Thirsk because if she stayed, she was afraid she might try to understand what was being said— only a word here and there, and she would probably get them wrong.

When she got back George was in his chair again, reading a medical journal, and although he looked up and smiled he didn't tell her who the caller had been. Surely if it had been his mother or one of his Dutch friends he would have said? She stayed staring down at the pages of her magazine and wondered if it had been Corina.

There were so few patients for the rest of the week that Phoebe wasn't needed in the surgery. She picked fruit in the garden for Mrs Thirsk's jam-making, did the flowers and polished the silver. She was perched on a stepladder, carefully wiping the chandelier in the sitting room, when George came through from the surgery a few mornings later.

'Finished already?' She wobbled a bit and he went to hold the ladder.

'Yes—we'll have time to talk before I go out. There's something I must tell you, Phoebe.' The ladder wobbled again, this time because she was shaking with sudden fright that he was going to tell her something she didn't want to hear, and he stretched up to lift her down. His arms were round her when the front door was pushed open and Phoebe's ear caught the squeak of the old-fashioned latch and looked over her shoulder through the open sitting-room door. Corina was in the hall walking towards them.

CHAPTER NINE

PHOEBE felt George's hands tighten round her waist and then lift her without haste to the ground. His easy, 'Hullo, Corina, what brings you here?' was uttered in a voice that betrayed neither surprise or annoyance.

Corina flung herself at him, wreathed her arms round his neck and kissed him. Only then did she say carelessly: 'Hullo, Phoebe,' before turning her attention to George once more. 'I got bored with Kasper—I sent him back to Holland; I decided I'd come and visit you again . . .' She began to talk in Dutch, and although George had removed her arms from around his neck, he listened with a half-amused smile. When she paused for breath he said over his shoulder to Phoebe: 'Can we put Corina up for a few days, my dear?'

Phoebe said from a dry mouth: 'Of course—there's a room ready. How nice to have her back again.' She added for good measure: 'For as long as she likes to say she can stay.'

George's firm mouth quivered very slightly. 'How did you get here?' he asked Corina.

'Oh, train and a taxi—it's still outside.'

He went out to see about her luggage and she called after him: 'Be a darling and pay him, George,' before she turned to Phoebe. 'Have I surprised you?' she asked. 'Probably not, you must have guessed that I don't give up easily.'

Phoebe crushed an impulse to slap the girl's face. 'Do come up to your room,' she said sweetly. 'Did you manage to buy any clothes? I'm afraid they'll be wasted here; we're all a bit old-fashioned.'

Corina, following her upstairs, giggled. 'George isn't—or hadn't you discovered that yet?'

A remark to be ignored. Phoebe opened the door of the room that Corina had had previously. 'Come down when you're ready,' she invited, 'the coffee will be just about ready by then.'

She met George in the hall, surrounded by expensive luggage.

'Rather a surprise,' he observed placidly.

She paused. 'For me, yes, but not, I imagine, for you.'

She saw his face become a bland mask. 'Will you explain that?' he asked her silkily.

'You had a phone call in Dutch—you didn't tell me who it was. Now I know.'

She went past him to the kitchen, ignoring his thunderous look.

Mrs Thirsk tut-tutted when she told her. 'More lamb chops,' she said at once, 'and there won't be enough peas.'

'I'll go down to the village as soon as I've had some coffee,' promised Phoebe. 'The doctor's not busy this morning—Juffrouw van Renkel won't be lonely.'

Her tone was so waspish that Mrs Thirsk paused in what she was doing to take a look at her. 'I can send Susan,' she suggested.

'No, I'll go—Susan's got the dining room to turn out, hasn't she?'

Phoebe picked up the tray and went back to the sitting room and plonked it down on the table by the window. George had gone out into the garden, Beauty at his heels, and she went into the hall when she heard Corina's voice.

'Send George up with my overnight bag, Phoebe, will you? I must do something to my face.'

'He's in the garden. Your stuff is in the hall, why not come down and get what you want? We're going to have coffee, so don't be too long.' Phoebe added gently: 'I don't suppose it matters too much about your face—it's only us here.'

She went back into the sitting room, not listening to Corina's cross mutterings and her indignant footsteps on the stairs.

Phoebe, looking at a portrait of one of George's ancestors, said softly: 'I'm behaving in the most shocking manner, and I'm not a bit sorry.'

The ancestor gazed back at her from eyes as blue as George's, and for one bemused moment Phoebe could have sworn that he winked at her. Imagined or not, it heartened her for George's return. 'Would you like to wait for your coffee?' she asked him pleasantly. 'I don't suppose Corina will be long.'

He stared at her and her insides went cold at the icy anger in his face. 'In that case, I'll wait.'

'O.K. You won't mind if I pop down to the village? We need more chops, you know, and a few other extras. I'll be back by the time Corina is ready.'

She had no intention of hurrying back. She sauntered along to the butcher's, purchased her chops, added peas and cream from Mrs Pratt and lingered to look in the antique shop; there was a charming little footstool she fancied. Old Mr Briggs, who owned the shop, was in the window arranging a French secretaire in one corner, and they smiled and waved to each other before she walked on. It was her birthday in a few days' time and she thought wistfully that birthdays for her had never meant much, with no family to send her cards, besides she had always avoided telling her few friends at the hospital for fear that they would pity her. George certainly didn't know, although she knew the date of his; his mother had told her. It would be nice to see Mrs Pritchard again.

She had taken longer than she should have done. She took her purchases to the kitchen and went along to the sitting room to apologise and drink her coffee. 'The freezer is being de-frosted,' she explained, 'so we've only got the minimum of food in the house for a couple of days.'

She realised as she spoke that Corina couldn't have cared less. She said: 'How boring for you,' and turned back to George. 'You cannot be busy all day,' she explained. 'Besides, I am your guest, and you must entertain me.' She opened her lovely eyes wide and added: 'Oh, George, you always used to entertain me.'

'Did I? I've forgotten.' He got to his feet. 'I'm off. I'll be back for lunch, Phoebe.' He bent and kissed her cheek, lifted a casual hand towards Corina and went away.

Which left the two girls facing each other over the coffee cups. 'Have you any plans?' asked Phoebe politely. 'There's not much to do, I'm afraid.'

'I will be all right.' Corina smiled widely at her. 'I will be—how do you say?—one of the family.'

The rest of the day was a nightmare to Phoebe, with Corina's ceaseless chat about clothes and make-up, only interrupted when George came home, when she transferred her attention solely to him. Phoebe, eyeing the cases lying around in Corina's bedroom, thought gloomily that her stay was going to be a long one. Corina had given no hint as to how long it might be, and since she had only just arrived, it would hardly do to enquire. She resolved to ask George when she had a little time with him.

Something easier said than done. He went to his study on the plea of work to be done after dinner that evening, and since by eleven o'clock he hadn't rejoined them, there was nothing to do but to suggest to Corina that they might go to bed. Something which she didn't want to do, but since Phoebe showed no sign of going upstairs without her, she gave in ungraciously enough and they went together, wishing each other an insincere goodnight at the head of the stairs. Phoebe, her ears stretched as she got ready for bed, heard George come up much later and go to his room. Even then she lay awake for another hour or more, listening to the familiar sounds of the old house settling for the night; creaks and rattles and the trees rustling against the side of the house, but nothing else. She slept at last, to wake early and go downstairs and make tea before Mrs Thirsk was up.

Corina didn't come down to breakfast. Mrs Thirsk, clearing the table once George had gone to the surgery, paused in her work.

'Would you be wanting me to take a tray up to the young lady?' she asked. 'Susan's not coming until ten o'clock and I've the lunch to see to . . .'

'No, there's no need', said Phoebe firmly. 'Juffrouw van Renkel knows when we have breakfast and I explained that if she didn't come down, there would be coffee when the surgery was over.'

Mrs Thirsk nodded briskly: 'Just so that I know, madam. You'll be going to help the doctor?'

'Yes, I think I'd better, the waiting room is pretty full. I'll make the beds afterwards and Susan can tidy upstairs when she comes. If Juffrouw van Renkel comes down before I get back into the house, will you tell her there are chairs out in the garden if she'd like to sit there.'

She hurried into the waiting room and started on the cards. George had found the first two or three for himself, but there were another half dozen for her to find. He thanked her politely when she got them and took them in, then asked her to dress a varicose ulcer and make several appointments; all in his pleasant manner, just as he had been pleasant at breakfast, a nasty cold pleasantness which had left her uncertain and miserable.

She dealt with the ulcer, made the appointments and went back into the waiting room. Well, two could play at that game, she told herself crossly. The moment the tiresome Corina took herself off—and let it be soon—she would have it out with him. She had thought she would be able to cope, loving him and hiding her feelings and behaving as before, but she could see now that it wouldn't work out. At least, not with Corina in the house. She took in the last patient's card and went back into the house, to find Corina strolling round, looking cross.

'I've had no breakfast,' she complained, 'and that woman said I'd have to wait for coffee. Really, I should have thought someone would have brought me a tray to my room.'

'Then you thought wrong,' said Phoebe sharply. 'Mrs Thirsk has enough to do in the mornings without carrying trays upstairs, and I'm busy in the surgery. I'm afraid if you can't come down to breakfast, you'll just have to wait until we have coffee.'

Corina opened her eyes wide. 'Why, Phoebe, how cross you sound! Anyone would think you don't want me here.'

Phoebe said unforgivably: 'Well, I don't remember inviting you,' and went off upstairs to
make the beds. When she got back again, George
was in the sitting room, noting his visits, and
Corina was perched on the side of the rent table,
with her legs swinging. That she had been talking
about Phoebe was obvious from the look of
triumph she shot at her as she went into the room.
She said at once in a little girl voice: 'You see,
George, how cross Phoebe looks. She doesn't want
me to stay—she said she hadn't invited me . . .'

He looked up briefly: 'You've already said that,
Corina, and I'm quite sure that if Phoebe did say
that she didn't mean it. My wife would never be
inhospitable to our guests.' His voice hardened.
'And if she did, I'm sure it was inadvertent and
she'll apologise.'

Phoebe stood very still looking at him. He
meant it, and she couldn't for the moment think of
anything to do other than that. She said in a voice
totally devoid of expression: 'I'm sorry—I have no
wish to be inhospitable, but perhaps Corina will
understand that carrying trays up to her bedroom
is a little difficult. Mrs Thirsk is far too busy. Of
course, I could leave the surgery while Corina is
here. That's up to you, George.'

She glared at him and was struck by the
ridiculous idea that he was laughing at her behind
his bland face. 'I'm sure Corina will fit in with our
busy mornings,' he said smoothly. 'And how
about that coffee?'

He didn't seem in the least put out. Phoebe,
handing cups, would have liked to have thrown
something at him. And at Corina, smiling a
satisfied little smile.

The next few days passed in an uneasy truce.
Corina made no more efforts to have her own

way, but she needled Phoebe whenever she had the chance. Then she criticised the food, always with a deprecating smile, complained gently that she couldn't sleep at night, that it was too hot to sit in the garden, too boring to go for a walk, too tiring to read. Phoebe made suitable replies and forbore to suggest that her guest might find life more exciting if she went back home. Almost a week had gone by and there was no mention of her leaving; almost a week in which Phoebe had had no chance at all to have George to herself. The only time they were alone was at breakfast, when he was immersed in his post, checking his visits and his diary, and interspersing this with a few polite remarks about the weather, calculated to reduce her to tonguetied silence and the briefest of monosyllables. This was a George she hadn't known about. Gone was the placid friendliness and ease of old friends; the cool politeness with which he treated her was more than she could bear. If they could have had just half an hour in which to talk—but somehow Corina was always there, taking the conversation into her own hands, begging prettily to be taken in the car when he paid his visits and pouting just as prettily when he refused.

'Well, since you are so disagreeable about it, George, I shall not ask you again, but at least you can take me somewhere interesting. I heard you say you were free on Saturday. Take me to Cambridge, I want to buy things and this funny little village of yours has nothing, and there is a restaurant there, Kasper told me about it—the Oyster Tavern. We'll lunch there and I'll shop, and in the evening we'll dine and dance.'

They were sitting in the garden after tea. Surgery was still an hour away and George was lying back, doing nothing, and so was Corina. Only Phoebe was sitting upright, knitting away like the furies.

'What do you say to that, Phoebe?' asked George. He spoke casually, but he had his eyes set on her face.

Before she could answer Corina spoke. 'Phoebe will be glad to have the house to herself for a few hours—besides, three is a horrid number.'

George had taken no notice of her at all. 'Phoebe?' he asked.

'I think it sounds fun, I'd like to go—we haven't been out much lately.'

Corina gave him a very direct look. 'Is there anyone we could rustle up for Phoebe?'

George's mouth twitched. 'Not offhand—all our friends are happily married and like to go out together.'

'Well then, we won't go,' declared Corina sulkily.

'But of course we'll go. You'll like Cambridge and there are some beautiful buildings—the colleges, you know.'

Corina said something in Dutch and got to her feet. 'I'm too hot, I shall sit indoors.' She got to her feet and said something, still in Dutch, to George. Her voice, Phoebe had to admit, was very beguiling.

'No, thanks,' said George, 'I'm very comfortable here.' He closed his eyes as she spoke and she flounced away.

'Phoebe,' said George, and his voice was so gentle that she dropped her knitting in a muddled heap to look at him. 'Phoebe, darling Phoebe . . .' and then, 'Oh, damn!' as the telephone rang.

He got up to answer it, leaving her to pick up her knitting and muddle through a row while she

digested the fact that he had called her darling. A
slip of the tongue? A softening up so that she
would agree to stay at home on Saturday? She
could hardly wait for him to come back so that she
could find out.

Only he didn't return, except for a few seconds to
say that he was going out to Pake's farm. 'Old Mrs
Pake had a coronary. Don't wait supper—I'll have
to go with her to the hospital. Tell any of the patients
who come to surgery to please come back later.'

His voice was brisk and he went away again
without a backward glance. Perhaps she had
dreamt the whole small episode.

He wasn't back for supper. It was after nine
o'clock when he got in and there were several
diehards in the waiting room, determined to be
seen even if they waited all night. It was another
half hour or so before he came into the house, and
Phoebe handed him a whisky before going to the
kitchen, to return in a moment with the soup
tureen and Mrs Thirsk following with cold beef
and jacket potatoes and salad. Corina, who had
sulked for most of the evening, followed her into
the dining room and sat down beside George at
the table, breaking into a flow of light chatter.
'Poor George—why do you do such a dreary job
when you could live so comfortably without doing
anything at all? All these sick people!' She made a
little face and Phoebe looked away. She knew how
George felt about his work; he would cheerfully
give up every penny of his wealth if it were a
question of that or his job. She wasn't surprised to
hear his noncommittal grunt, and it cheered her
enormously.

He was tired. She looked at him lovingly, seeing
the lines etched on his calm face. She asked
quietly: 'Were you in time?'

He nodded. 'I hope so. Old Pake's badly shaken.'

'I'll cycle out there in the morning, if you think that might help?'

'Will you? I think it might. There's a daughter coming tomorrow about midday.'

'I'll stay till she comes. I can go directly after surgery.'

He nodded and then turned courteously to Corina, who was asking him something in Dutch.

'Oh, no, no fear of that. I'll still have Saturday free—Andrew takes over for me.'

Mrs Thirsk came in with fresh coffee and Phoebe helped her clear the table while the others went into the drawing room. When she joined them, George was in his chair, going through his afternoon post, and Corina was sitting on one of the sofas doing nothing. Perhaps, thought Phoebe hopefully, she would go to bed.

But she didn't. She stayed there, rather silent for once, making conversation difficult, until George said: 'What about an early night?' and stood up and wished them a cheerful goodnight which they couldn't ignore.

Morning surgery wasn't busy. Phoebe did what was necessary there and got on her bike. It was a couple of miles to Pake's farm and a flat road all the way. Once she was there, she was kept busy, making up a bed for the daughter, getting old Mr Pake some kind of late breakfast, reassuring him about his wife, and then preparing some sort of a meal against the daughter's arrival. She was tired as she cycled slowly back home; the daughter had arrived, a nice, sensible woman who thanked her while she was putting on an apron. 'We'll be fine now, Mrs Pritchard, I've no doubt the doctor will be out to see us some time.'

Phoebe played a game with herself all the way home, pretending that Corina would be gone by the time she got there, but it was only a game. The girl was still there, all right, curled up on the sofa, doing nothing as usual, magazines scattered round and an empty coffee cup on the floor. Phoebe picked it up, wished her good morning and went to confer with Mrs Thirsk about lunch.

George had been his usual calm self at breakfast. Crumbling toast opposite him, Phoebe had waited hopefully for him to call her darling once again, but he hadn't, only made some prosaic remark about the Pake family and gone into the surgery. There was no sign of him now and this afternoon he had a meeting at the hospital at Bury St Edmunds. She sighed, seeing no hope of talking to him.

He was back for lunch but away again directly they had finished, taking no notice of Corina's grumbles that she was bored with doing nothing. 'I mean to say,' she said pettishly, 'Phoebe hasn't got a car, she can't even drive.'

'She's hardly had the time to learn,' George pointed out reasonably. 'What's wrong with a bike?'

Corina hunched a shoulder. 'In this heat? Besides, where would I go?'

'I'll be back for evening surgery,' said George, and went.

The afternoon lasted for ever; Phoebe thanked heaven for a full waiting room after tea to keep her busy until supper time.

To her surprise Corina joined them for breakfast the next morning, dressed ready for their trip to Cambridge—a sleeveless dress of wild silk and a little jacket to match, calculated to take her through the day—without the jacket the dress would be just right for dinner and dancing. Phoebe, still in a cotton dress, mentally assessed her wardrobe to see if she could do better.

'We'll leave at ten o'clock,' said George, and went to his study, while Corina disposed herself carefully in a chair in the sitting room and Phoebe cleared the table and then went upstairs to change her dress.

She had plenty of clothes to choose from. She chose a pale blue crepon, very plain and very understated chic. She did her hair and face once again, found a little blue cashmere jacket to go with the dress and went downstairs as George came out of the study.

He didn't say anything, but crossed the hall to kiss her quickly and then, still not speaking, opened the house door. Phoebe, a bit flustered by the kiss, went to say goodbye to Mrs Thirsk and Susan and then went out to the car. It was too much to expect that Corina would have got into the back of the car. She was already curled up beside George.

They were a bare five miles from Woolpit, on the main road travelling fast, when the car phone buzzed. George slowed and picked up the receiver and then stopped, listening intently. Finally he said, 'I'm on my way,' turned the car and went back even faster than they had come.

'Why have you turned round?' demanded Corina. 'We're going to Cambridge. You promised!'

He took no notice of her. Over his shoulder he said: 'That was Andrew—he's out on a baby case and he can't get back. The two Arkwright boys, Mrs Biggs' youngest and little Tracy Bunting have eaten Laburnum seeds. Mrs Bunting found some in Tracy's hand.'

He didn't expect an answer, and Phoebe didn't

speak, thankful that his bag was in the car. It was Corina who broke the silence. 'George, I want to go to Cambridge. You don't have to go back; it's your day off . . .'

They were going down Woolpit's main street and he didn't answer her but stopped outside a row of cottages at the end of the village, reached for his bag and got out of the car. The door of the end cottage was open and there was a group of women outside it. George went past them through the door and Phoebe followed him; four small children, all most likely very ill and three mothers besides themselves—he would need help. She smiled a little at the women clustered round the door and found George in the small front room, made even smaller by his bulk and the four little creatures lying on their distraught mothers' laps. He was already bending over Tracy. 'Get the syringes out of my bag, Phoebe,' his voice was calm and unhurried, 'then get the other three on to their sides—we must try and make them sick and clear their airways.' After a moment he said: 'When you've done that get on the phone. I want two ambulances here, fast. Someone may have phoned—if so hurry them up.'

No one had phoned, they had all been too panicky; someone had had the sense to ring the surgery and it was Mrs Thirsk who had passed the message on to Andrew. Phoebe met her coming down the street as she ran over to the Post Office and banged on the door. Saturday morning, and most of the village off to Stowmarket for shopping and Mrs Pratt not opening the shop at all.

'The phone,' said Phoebe breathlessly when she opened the door, and darted past her.

The children were semi-conscious. The two boys had been sick and looked decidedly better, but

Tracy and Mrs Biggs' little boy looked dreadful.
Phoebe did the things George bade her to while
Mrs Thirsk went to the kitchen and made tea for
the mothers, and they had barely finished it when
the ambulances arrived. 'I'll go with Tracy and
Benny Biggs,' said George. 'You go with the
Arkwrights. The mothers had better come too.' He
called to Mrs Thirsk: 'Make sure someone looks
after the other children.'

He picked up Tracy and went out to the
ambulance, handed over Benny to the ambulance
man, urged the mothers in and got in himself.

Phoebe did the same, vaguely aware that Corina
was calling angrily for George from the car, but
far too preoccupied to listen.

At the hospital the children were whisked away
and Phoebe sat down to wait for George. He came
half an hour later, shepherding the three mothers.
'Now to get back home,' he said cheerfully.
'They're all right—a few days here and they'll be
home again. I'll see if I can get a taxi.'

But there was no need; the car was outside in
the forecourt with Mr Platt at the wheel. 'Mrs
Thirsk told me to come after you, sir. I hope I did
right ...'

'Indeed you did, bless you both. It'll be a
squeeze, but I daresay we can manage. You three
ladies get in the back; Phoebe in the front between
us.'

It was a squash, but no one minded. Mr Platt
and the three women got out at the bottom of the
village and George drove on up to his own house.

They could hear Corina as they went in and she
came racing down the stairs as they stood in the
hall. 'I won't stay another minute here!' she
screamed at them. 'Look at you, Phoebe—you're
filthy—your dress, it's disgusting—don't come

near me! Of all the beastly ways of living . . .' She rounded on George, standing quietly an arm on Phoebe's shoulder.

'I never want to see you again!' she screeched. 'I thought it would be fun to get you away from Phoebe, but you can have her! You can bring my bags down, there's a taxi coming for me, I can't get away from here fast enough.' She glared at Phoebe. 'You smell abominable!' she snapped.

George laughed. His arm tightened round Phoebe and he bent to kiss her flushed face. 'Go and get cleaned up,' he suggested. 'I'll see our guest off the premises.'

Phoebe heard Corina's outraged gasp as she sped upstairs, to find Mrs Thirsk already there, running a bath and arranging a pile of towels. 'All ready, Mrs Pritchard, and just you give me that dress, it'd better go into the dustbin, it's past saving. Still, what's a dress . . . they're all right, the children?'

'Yes, Mrs Thirsk.' Phoebe was tearing off her clothes. 'Is Juffrouw van Renkel really going? Has she packed?'

'Lord bless you, Mrs Pritchard, that she has—got me to get a taxi for her too. Going home, she told me, never wants to come here again.' Mrs Thirsk came out of the bedroom and poked her head round the bathroom door and addressed Phoebe's head sticking out of the bath water. 'In a bit of a taking, if I might say so. Shall I lay out some clothes for the doctor?'

'Please, Mrs Thirsk, he's just as filthy as I am. Do you suppose we could have some sort of meal? I know we're supposed to be out, but is there anything cold—sandwiches, perhaps?'

'Leave it to me, ma'am,' said Mrs Thirsk, and bustled away.

Phoebe, fresh from her bath, her mousy hair washed and hanging loose to dry, put on a sleeveless dress and some rather dashing sandals and went downstairs. Corina must have gone by now and she supposed George was in his room. There was no one in the sitting room, nor in the dining room, and the drawing room was empty. For an awful moment she stood in the hall, not allowing herself to think that George had perhaps driven Corina to wherever she wanted to go. She went slowly to the house door and opened it to look out. The car wasn't there and she let out a small wailing: 'Oh, George!'

She gave a squeak as his arms went round her. 'Still determined to think the worst of me?' he asked softly, and twirled her round to face him.

She stared up at him. 'Yes—no—that is, where's Corina?'

'Gone. I forgot to ask her where.' He added tenderly: 'What a goose you are, my darling. I was always under the impression that a girl knew when a man was in love with her—you're the exception to the rule.'

'How would I know?' she said with a snap. 'No one's been in love with me.' She suddenly burst into tears. 'Oh, George, I wish you were . . .' She gave a great gulp. 'Oh, I didn't mean to say that.'

'But you said it, and you can't unsay it. Lord, I began to think we were destined to be good friends for life—I couldn't have kept it up much longer.'

'Kept up what?'

'Why, the pretence of being just a friend, when I've been in love with you for ever—since we met, at any rate.'

Phoebe felt a pleasant tingle of excitement. 'You never said . . .' she began.

'Of course not, you would have turned tail and run away.' He bent and kissed her. 'Dear heart.'

No one had ever called her that before, it made her feel a little dizzy. All the same, she said severely: 'What about Corina?'

'I've known her most of my life and not liked her overmuch, but our families were friendly and we went out and about—oh, years ago. And when she turned up at Mother's house, it seemed to me to be a good idea to make you jealous.'

'Oh, I was, and when she came here with Kasper . . . and then coming again like that, I thought that you—that she . . . that phone call.'

'No, my love, I don't care two straws for her. And the phone call was from Grandmother. I didn't tell you because I was angry that you took it for granted that it was Corina.'

He caught her very close so that she could barely breathe. 'My dear darling, we shall be so happy, you and I and a houseful of children. You won't find it dull?'

'Dull?' said Phoebe. 'Dull? Oh, George, how could it be dull with you?' She kissed him gently, already savouring the delightful future stretching endlessly. She smiled up at him and he kissed her back, not gently at all, so that she trembled with the delight of it.

Mrs Thirsk, crossing the hall on the way to the sitting room with a tray of coffee, came to a soundless halt, turned on her heel and went back to the kitchen. At Susan's look of enquiry she said happily: 'They won't be wanting coffee just yet, they've got other things to think about. And don't you dare go into the hall, my girl, not till I say so.'

Susan peeled another potato. 'Happen they're in love,' she said.

'Happen they are.' Mrs Thirsk smiled broadly. 'And high time too.'

Here's how to get this special offer from Harlequin! As simple as 1...2...3!

AUGUST
TREASURY EDITION
COUPON

1. Each month, save one Treasury Edition coupon from your favorite Romance or Presents novel.
2. In four months you'll have saved four Treasury Edition coupons (only one coupon per month allowed).
3. Then all you have to do is fill out and return the order form provided, along with the four Treasury Edition coupons required and $1.00 for postage and handling.

RT1-A-2

Mail to: Harlequin Reader Service

In the U.S.A.
P.O. Box 52040
Phoenix, AZ 85072-2040

In Canada
P.O. Box 2800, Postal Station A
5170 Yonge Street
Willowdale, Ont. M2N 6J3

Please send me my FREE copy of the Janet Dailey Treasury Edition. I have enclosed the four Treasury Edition coupons required and $1.00 for postage and handling along with this order form.

(Please Print)

NAME_____

ADDRESS_____

CITY_____

STATE/PROV._____ ZIP/POSTAL CODE_____

SIGNATURE_____

This offer is limited to one order per household.

SUPPLIES LIMITED

This special Janet Dailey offer expires January 1986.

You're invited to accept 4 books and a surprise gift Free!

Acceptance Card

Mail to: **Harlequin Reader Service®**

In the U.S.
2504 West Southern Ave.
Tempe, AZ 85282

In Canada
P.O. Box 2800, Postal Station A
5170 Yonge Street
Willowdale, Ontario M2N 6J3

YES! Please send me 4 free Harlequin Romance® novels and my free surprise gift. Then send me 6 brand new novels every month as they come off the presses. Bill me at the low price of $1.65 each ($1.75 in Canada)—an 11% saving off the retail price. There are no shipping, handling or other hidden costs. There is no minimum number of books I must purchase. I can always return a shipment and cancel at any time. Even if I never buy another book from Harlequin, the 4 free novels and the surprise gift are mine to keep forever.   116 BPR-BPGE

Name	(PLEASE PRINT)

Address	Apt. No.

City	State/Prov.	Zip/Postal Code

This offer is limited to one order per household and not valid to present subscribers. Price is subject to change.   ACR-SUB-1